HORSE  RESCUE:

TREASURE

BY

WHITNEY SANDERSON

In memory of Treasure

Text copyright © 2015 by Whitney Sanderson
Cover and chapter head illustrations © 2015 by Ruth Sanderson

Visit us on the web:
www.whitneysanderson.com
www.thelittlebrookfarm.org
www.goldenwoodstudio.com

Printed by CreateSpace, An Amazon.com Company
Charleston, SC

First Edition

TABLE OF CONTENTS

CHAPTER ONE

The Auction

Sweat trickled down my coat as I waited in the crowded pen with the other auction horses. The bruised-looking clouds seemed ready to spill over, and I jumped in my skin as lightning flashed across the sky. My instinct told me to flee from the storm, to seek shelter. But there was nowhere to run.

Opal stood beside me, pressed against the metal bars of the corral. I stayed close to her side to protect her from being jostled. She had stepped on a nail last night, and now she was lame. The people who'd come to throw us pitchforks full of hay from the back of a pickup truck hadn't noticed she was injured. Now she held up her foreleg to keep from driving the nail deeper into her hoof. I could tell from her ragged breathing that she was in pain.

I remembered how Opal's coat had gleamed like moonlight at the Parents' Day show last summer, before we had spent the winter together in a horse trader's pasture, waiting for the next camp season. Opal was gray, but with a warm tone to her coat like she was standing in sunlight, no matter the weather. Now her fur was the same dark, dirty color as the clouds above us. All the horses were covered in dust. We kicked it up with our churning hooves and breathed it in so it coated our throats.

There was a rusty trough in the corner, but the water was warm and muddy. Some of the other horses had green slime running from their noses, and they drank from the same tub. I was thirsty, but not enough to drink that filthy water.

The thunder's getting closer, said Opal. *I hope Olivia brings me inside soon. My braids will get ruined if it rains.* Olivia had been Opal's favorite rider at Camp Friendship. Together they'd taken first prize in nearly all of the gymkhana games.

Opal blinked and seemed to notice where she was. *What will happen to us now, Treasure?* she said. *Do you think they'll sell us together?*

I touched my nose to hers in reassurance. But I didn't feel certain at all. Opal's skin was burning up. She needed a vet, but there wasn't one here. The best we could hope for was to be sold quickly.

At first I had believed the children who whispered in my ear that they'd take me home with them at the end of the summer. But they never did. Every August I would find myself bound for another auction, another winter in a rough pasture with too little hay shared between too many horses. As soon as the grass got green again I would be sent to another auction and probably a new camp. There, new girls would fall in love with me and cry into my mane when they had to go home.

At auction, the best thing was to be bought by a family who wanted a trail horse or a 4-H project for their children. These buyers picked the youngest, healthiest, most obedient animals. The horses that weren't quite as pretty or well-trained went mostly to lesson stables or summer camps, which was where I had always gone. The horses that the camps didn't want were the unluckiest of all.

Several horses had already been loaded into the slat-sided metal trailer that was bound for the slaughterhouse. First had been a blind gelding, then a mare who was nearly bald with rain rot, and just a few minutes ago, a scruffy fleabitten pony who pinned his ears and sunk his teeth into the arm of the man who led him. I didn't know exactly what happened at the slaughterhouse, but no horse who'd been sent there had ever come back.

The magnified voice of the auctioneer crackled from inside the covered arena. Every few minutes another horse was led through the double doors. The auction had been going on since early this morning. The horses that remained were increasingly restless, not knowing their fates.

Opal, I said to my companion, *When they bring you inside, you must try not to limp or look sick. Even if it makes your leg hurt. It's very important.*

Opal didn't answer. Her body trembled and her jaw seemed to be clenched shut. Suddenly it began to rain, the drops stinging my skin. As hot as it had been just minutes before, I was soon soaked and shivering.

Just then, a weanling colt saw his mother being led to the arena. He reared up and crashed against me, his sharp hooves slicing my shoulder. Opal squealed with pain as she was jostled onto her bad leg. I nipped at the colt's neck, warning him to keep his distance, but I couldn't work up much anger. He was as lost as we were.

A teenage boy wearing a plastic rain slicker entered the pen and clipped a lead rope to my halter. I stood stubbornly still, not wanting to leave Opal. The boy tugged insistently, but I dug my heels into the ground.

Wouldn't do that if I were you, a skinny gelding drawled from nearby. *Never give 'em an excuse to whip you.*

Opal looked at me with feverish eyes. *Go on, Trea-*

sure, she said. *We have to obey our handlers. The kids could get hurt, you know, if you act up.*

The boy was still yanking at my halter. I was stronger than any person, but men had whips and blindfolds and sooner or later they always got their way. With a last despairing whinny to Opal, I bolted through the open gate, dragging my handler along behind me.

It was dim and shadowy inside the arena, even with the artificial lights that glared down. My nose and ears were filled with strange smells and sounds before my eyes could adjust. I caught the scent of humans and the greasy foods they ate. I heard the drone of the auctioneer over the loudspeaker.

Soon I made out the shapes of a dozen people gathered near the temporary fence that separated the horses from the bidders. It was a small crowd this year. I didn't see any of the buyers I recognized from past camps.

My handler dragged me down the auction chute, then clucked to me to trot back the other way. I obeyed numbly, rolling my eyes at the boy's flapping rain slicker and the waving hands of the audience.

The boy halted me in front of the auctioneer's stand, and I noticed a dark-haired woman and a young girl watching me from the crowd.

"She looks like a sweet mare," said the girl. "With that face, she could be part Arabian. Can we bid on her?"

I arched my neck and tried to look spirited and healthy, even though I felt skittish and exhausted and the cut on my shoulder stung.

The woman looked me up and down. "We have to be careful," she said. "Some of the horses here have strangles, and we can't take the risk of infecting the rest of our herd."

"I don't think she's sick," said the girl. "Her eyes are so bright. She hasn't given up like some of the others."

"You know we only have enough money to buy one horse today, Summer," the woman replied. The girl bit her lip and said something I couldn't hear over the crackle of the microphone.

"Horse number seventy, a ten-year-old grade mare." The auctioneer's voice boomed across the arena. "Fourteen-point-one hands, broke to ride. She was at Camp Friendship last summer and her name is Treasure. Who'll start the bidding at two hundred and fifty dollars?"

There was a pause while the woman and the girl talked in voices too low for me to hear. "Come on, folks," said the auctioneer. "I bet Treasure here would make a good first pony for the kids. Got a nice soft eye, this mare." There was a pleading note in his voice.

A man wearing a cowboy hat and a sweat-stained plaid shirt paused to take a bite of a dripping hamburger. Then he raised a piece of paper with a number written on it.

The girl gasped. "That's the meat buyer, isn't it?" she said. The woman nodded grimly.

"I've got two-fifty," said the auctioneer, looking grim. "Do I hear three hundred?"

The woman raised her number, and the auctioneer sat up straighter.

"I hear three hundred. Who'll give me three-fifty, three-fifty for Treasure?"

The man in the cowboy hat polished off his

hamburger, then raised his bid.

"I hear three-fifty, three-fifty, who'll give me four…?"

The woman held up her number again.

"I hear four hundred, four hundred, who'll give me four twenty-five…?"

The man in the cowboy hat made a cutting motion across his throat.

"SOLD!" cried the auctioneer, "For four hundred dollars to bidder number fifteen. Congratulations, Lynn, she looks like a nice one."

The boy in the rain slicker led me out of the auction chute, where my new owners were waiting.

The girl took the rope from his hands and patted my neck. Her hair was long and reddish-gold. I reached out to nibble it, and the girl laughed.

"That's not hay!" she cried, tugging her hair out of my teeth. "But you probably don't remember what hay looks like, you're all skin and bones."

"Let's get her loaded, Summer," said the woman— it sounded like her name was Lynn. "We've got a long drive, and it's getting close to supper time for the horses."

"Okay, Mom." On our way out of the arena, we passed the man in the cowboy hat. He was leaning against the fence while he waited for the next horse to be brought in. He smelled like charred meat and smoke. I shied away from him as we passed.

Outside, lightning rippled across the sky. Rain was still pouring down by the bucketful. Lynn opened the back of a small trailer and I followed the girl, Summer, onboard. There was a net full of fresh hay, and I couldn't resist grabbing a mouthful despite my anxiety.

Near my head was a dusty window with a view of the parking lot, where other horses were being loaded up too. Some went willingly, but others resisted. People ran ropes behind their hindquarters to startle them forward.

I saw the man in the cowboy hat leading a gray mare toward the trailer that held other lame and sick horses. *Opal!* I called out to her, the sound echoing in the enclosed space. Her ears pricked briefly in my direction. She whinnied back. The man jerked on her halter, and she returned her attention to him. I kicked out at the walls of my trailer, but I was trapped.

The man leading Opal was impatient with her halting strides. He smacked the lead rope against her flanks to get her to move faster. She stopped at the edge of the massive stock trailer, peering nervously inside.

Opal, no! Don't get in! I neighed as loudly as I could. Dread flooded through me, icier than the rain. I knew the end awaiting the horses in that trailer was an awful one. My hooves drummed against the rubber floor mat so hard that the small vehicle swayed and shook.

Outside, the man in the cowboy hat cracked the rope again. Opal, always obedient, lowered her head and stepped onto the trailer. The last thing I saw was a huge metal door that swung shut and closed her into darkness.

The ground shifted underfoot as my own trailer pulled out of the parking lot. I hardly noticed the jostling as I was carried down one bumpy country road after another. Through my speckled window I could see flashes of houses with children playing in small yards, then cities with neon billboards and buildings that belched black smoke, then pastures full of grazing sheep and cows.

With every mile I felt my distance from Opal increasing. My heart felt like a bucket with a hole in the bottom, and all my hope leaking out.

I had no idea where I was being taken, and I didn't care.

CHAPTER TWO

LITTLE BROOKFARM

The trailer shuddered to a halt and a car door slammed. A moment later, Summer ducked into the front of the trailer. The back opened and fresh air washed over me. Summer's mother dropped the bar behind my hindquarters. I backed out as quickly as I could, my hooves flailing through empty space before they reached the ground.

As soon as I was back on solid earth, I whirled around and scanned the horizon for danger. I was in a stable yard between a red barn and a white farmhouse. Dirt paddocks filled with horses surrounded the build-

WHITNEY SANDERSON

ings, and larger grassy pastures lay beyond. A dense forest bordered the farm on three sides, and the road lay on the fourth.

The barn doorway glowed with warm light, contrasting with the cold evening colors outside. Inside, the heads of several horses poked curiously over the half-doors of their stalls. Summer led me through the barn, down a concrete aisle to a freshly bedded stall at the very back of the stable. I was the only horse in this part of the barn.

Lynn carried over a brimming water bucket and hung it on a hook in the stall. I was thirsty, and I craned my neck toward the bucket. As soon as I stepped over the threshold a wave of fear swept over me. I stopped in my tracks.

I could smell the familiar stall scents of pine boards and sweet straw. But in my memory everything was black and burning. Smoke filled my lungs, and there was no escape …

I reared up in a panic, knocking Summer to the ground, and raced down the aisle toward freedom. I splashed across the muddy stable yard and skidded to a halt when I reached a fence.

My ribs heaved for air as Summer and her mother came out of the barn. They approached slowly, holding out their hands. The air was damp and fresh. The acrid scent of smoke was gone. The fire had only been in my imagination.

Even so, I dug my heels into the ground when Summer grabbed the end of my dangling lead rope. I couldn't go back inside, not when I knew I'd be trapped if the place really did start to burn.

Summer quickly realized that I wasn't going back into the stall. She led me past the barn and up a hill to an isolated paddock with a shed in one corner, a water trough in the other. Summer led me through the gate, slipped off my halter, and hung it on the gatepost.

I trotted around the fence line, eyeing the boards for soundness. The fence was tight, no way out. I sniffed the ground. Other horses had been here, but not recently.

The misting rain began to seep through my short

summer coat. I went into the shed, shivering to keep warm. I felt safer here than in a stall, knowing I could move freely in and out. Summer returned with two flakes of hay and a plaid turnout sheet. She buckled the blanket over my chest and under my belly while I grabbed a huge mouthful of hay.

"I wonder what happened to make you so scared of the barn," she said. "You don't have to be frightened here, though. No one will hurt you." She watched me eat for a few minutes, stroking my damp neck, then slipped back through the gate and went into the white house at the bottom of the hill. I could see through the open window that she and her mother were having their own dinner inside.

The hay disappeared all too quickly. I lipped the ground to pick up every wisp. It had been days since I'd eaten properly. Even though I had stayed outdoors through colder nights than this, I felt unusually chilled. All winter I'd had Opal beside me to keep warm. If only she were here now...

No, it didn't matter. I was used to looking out for

myself. As long as my owners gave me food and water, I'd be fine. The trick was to stay outside, where I could drink rain and nibble weeds if they forgot about me.

Being alone didn't matter, not really. Herds and friendship were fine if there was enough food, but I couldn't count on that. Surviving was all that mattered. I drank deeply from the trough, making sure to save enough water for tomorrow.

Then I stood in the shed with my nose pressed into one corner and my haunches turned to the outside. In this position, I could defend myself from any danger that might attack in the night.

The next morning a veterinarian came to examine me. It had been a long time since I'd seen a vet, but I remembered the antiseptic soap smell and the sting of injections. I had two shots today. They felt like bee stings, but I held still because I knew this was how humans protected us from disease. The soothing balm the vet spread onto my scraped shoulder felt nice, even though it smelled like chemicals too.

After the vet left, I hung my head over the paddock fence to watch the activities of the farm. Horses of all different sizes and breeds were turned out in the pastures. A black-and-white rooster strutted around like he owned the place, pecking around the horse's feed tubs for spilled grain. Half a dozen dogs trotted at people's heels or lay panting in the sun, and the place was teeming with cats.

Beyond the barn was a large arena filled with brightly painted jumps. I watched as Lynn gave lessons there for most of the day. Her students ranged from toddlers on ponies to daring teenagers who urged their horses over jumps made out of old tires and hay bales. One black gelding was particularly stunning. Summer rode him, and the pair seemed to attack the jumps as if they were riding into battle.

Later in the afternoon, a group of teenage girls led a large chestnut horse into the arena. They were dressed in thin tights and soft shoes that were different than the usual hard-soled riding boots, and they wore no helmets. The horse looked like a Warmblood, with a muscular neck and long elegant legs wrapped in leopard print polos. He wore a leather surcingle with handles in place of a saddle.

A girl in a silver sequined shirt set a radio down on the mounting block and began to play a song with an energetic beat. The other girls sat on the fence, watching while the girl in the sparkly shirt stood in the center of the arena.

The chestnut horse walked and trotted in circles around her on a long rope, I think it was called a longe line. The sight was familiar, but I had never experienced it myself. Riders usually only took the time to longe unruly mounts or fancy show horses. I was neither of these.

The gelding's handler signaled him to canter. His strides were slow and rhythmic. A short girl with curly brown hair jumped down off the fence and began to lope along at his side. She grabbed one of the surcingle handles and used the gelding's motion to launch herself up onto his back.

The gelding continued to canter as if this were

nothing out of the ordinary. The girl balanced on her knees on his broad back. She held one leg out straight behind her, toes pointed. Then she rose carefully to her feet and stretched her arms out to the side, keeping her knees slightly bent. Finally she did a handstand, holding on to the surcingle's handles.

Another girl came running up beside the horse and was swept onboard too. The pair of riders performed similar movements together, helping each other balance. When they had finished, the girl with curly hair swung her legs to the side, pushed herself away from the horse, and landed on her feet with a bounce.

The other girl did a backwards flip off the horse's rump. She landed on her feet too, and her friends applauded. During all this, the chestnut gelding never changed the rocking horse rhythm of his canter.

After the girls had put the gelding away, they came flocking up to my paddock and started hugging and fussing over me.

"What a sweet mare," said the girl in the sequined shirt. She vaulted lightly up onto my bare back. "Shhh, don't tell Lynn!" she said, laughing.

The girl who had done a backflip started braiding my forelock, while the one who was sitting on my back reached forward to massage the tight muscles of my neck. I began to warm up to the attention, nosing the girls' hands for treats. I wasn't disappointed—one of them found a striped peppermint in her pocket and fed it to me.

"Liz, what are you doing on that horse? Summer hasn't even ridder her yet!" Lynn called from the stable.

The girl in the sequined shirt quickly hopped down from my back. The group gave me a final shower of pats and then headed back toward the stable, doing handstands and cartwheels on the grassy slope.

Soon, cars full of parents returned to pick up the children. So this was just another camp, after all. Which meant that as nice as this place seemed, I couldn't count on staying here long.

I was kept apart from the other horses for two

WHITNEY SANDERSON

weeks. Summer or some of the other young riders came to visit me every day. Soon I got to know Liz, Jodi, Tara, Chrissy, Sean, and other girls and boys who lavished attention on me. They brushed my bay coat until it shone and combed the tangles out of my mane and tail.

Even the cats were friendly here. A gray tabby came strolling along the top of the fence and rubbed her head against my muzzle, purring.

Alhough I was well cared for, I felt restless. Was I going to stay in this paddock forever? Just then, Summer and her friend Chrissy came out of the barn with a set of tack.

"Hey, Treasure!" Summer called out. I flicked an ear, but it was more in response to the sound of her voice than to the name. I had only been called Treasure for the past year.

When camp horses were sent to auction, sometimes no one would bother to write down their names. At different barns I had been called Feather, Belle, Mabel, and Duchess.

"Your Coggins test came back, and you've got a clean bill of health from Dr. Fallon," said Summer, setting the saddle down on the fence. "Now it's time to see how much training you've had."

Chrissy tied me to a post in the shed with a safety-release knot that could be loosened in one motion if I started to panic. I was relieved when the girls tightened my girth slowly instead of yanking it, and grateful that they how to put my on bridle properly. One inexperienced camper had nearly strangled me by fastening my throatlatch too tightly.

Summer and Chrissy led me down to the arena. Chrissy sat on the mounting block while Summer put me through my paces. She walked, trotted, and cantered me in both directions. I knew the lesson routine, and I tried to follow her signals willingly.

The first time she sat back to ask me to walk, I flung up my head to evade the harsh pull of the bit I'd come to expect. But Summer's hands were soft, and she mostly used her seat and legs to cue me. She was a better rider than I was used to. Many of the campers who'd ridden

27

me had seemed to be asking me to turn left and right at the same time, or slow down and go faster all at once.

Summer trotted me in a circle, then aimed me at a cross-rail in the center of the arena. I hopped over the tiny fence. Summer asked me to canter on to a vertical about two feet high. This time my hoof clipped the rail and brought it down. I twitched my tail in irritation.

Chrissy fixed the jump, and Summer circled me toward it again. She leaned forward and released the reins as we reached the base of the fence, but I didn't feel ready for takeoff. I skidded to a halt, nearly crashing into the raised pole.

Summer fell forward onto my neck, but quickly pushed herself back into the saddle. She circled me around for another try. This time I rushed the fence and took off a stride too early. My hind legs caught the rail and sent it clattering down.

Summer had me try the fence twice more. Even though I pushed off as hard as I could, the rail fell both times. Summer took me over the cross-rail again. I jumped it easily. I started to aim toward the higher fence, but Summer drew me back to a walk.

"She's quiet and responsive on the flat," Summer said to Chrissy. "Her mouth's a little tough, though, and she seems to have trouble clearing the fences."

"She doesn't really have the conformation for jumping, does she?" said Chrissy, eyeing me critically. "Her shoulder is too straight, and she's got a pretty bad swayback. Are you sure she's only ten years old? Maybe the people at the auction lied."

"No, Dr. Fallon looked at her teeth. She said they're not worn down like an older horse's would be. Her swayback is probably a conformation fault she was born with. Or else someone rode her when she was too young, before her back was strong enough."

I chewed nervously at my bit. A swayback—did that mean they didn't want me? I broke into a trot and headed toward the jump again. I'd get over it somehow!

But Summer sat back in the saddle and made me walk. We circled the arena until I was cool. Afteward, Summer sponged me off on the lawn outside the barn and let me graze.

I expected to be returned to my lonely corral on the hill, but instead Summer brought me to a larger paddock near the barn. Inside, a fat pony was contorting her neck into an impossible shape to lip at some clover blossoms growing just out of reach under the fence.

Why is it that the greenest grass always the next pasture over? said the pony, sliding her head back between the rails. She peered at me from underneath a fuzzy forelock. White hairs mixed with the black ones on her face and legs, giving her a mottled roan appearance.

We touched our noses together to exchange greetings. The pony squealed and I drew back, startled. But then she reached out to nibble me in a friendly way.

Howdy, my name's Winnie, she said. *Looks like y'all are going to be my new paddock buddy.*

I guess so. I'm Treasure. I took another look at the little mare. Her beady eyes sparkled beneath her puff of forelock. Her rump was as round as an apple. It looked like I didn't have to worry about being fed here, anyway.

I've seen you up on yonder hill for the past few weeks.

They keep the new horses in quarantine there until the vet says they don't have swamp fever or strangles or anything contagious. Stuff like that can sweep through a herd faster than a loose horse through a bag of oats, you know?

Sure, I said uncertainly. I had never been in quarantine before. I was usually just unloaded into a field full of other horses who'd come from all corners of creation.

The rooster I had seen earlier strutted over, crowed loudly, and started pecking my hooves. I laid back my ears and pawed the ground.

Don't mind Duncan, said Winnie. *He doesn't have a proper flock o' hens right now. I figure he thinks us mares are a poor substitute. He tries to boss us around, but we don't pay him much mind. He's a plucky bird, though. He was living out in the wild and disturbin' the peace by cock-a-doodle-doo'ing every sunrise and waking folks up. The authorities tried to catch him, but good ol' Duncan gave them the slip for more than a month before they finally netted him.*

The rooster gazed coldly at me for a moment,

then walked away clucking and fanning his tail plumes. Well, he wouldn't be getting any of *my* grain. In my experience, roosters were right up there with coyotes and nanny goats on the list of animals to avoid associating with.

So what's your story, Treasure? said Winnie, sidling up to me so we could swat flies away from each other's faces with our tails. As if we'd known each other since we were suckling foals or something.

It's not very interesting, I said evasively, not wanting to share my life story with a horse I'd just met. I sidestepped out of range of Winnie's flicking tail.

Right, personal space, said Winnie, looking hurt. *Gotcha. I just figured since the bugs are real bad...*

It's okay, I said. *I'm still just getting used to everything. What is this place?*

It's a horse rescue farm. Lynn and her daughter Summer run the place, with a lot of help from volunteers. They take in horses from all kinds of bad situations.

For how long? I asked.

Why, forever, unless Lynn finds the perfect home

for them.

I snorted. At camp, all the horses would talk about the day when the Perfect Owner would come along. They imagined that their favorite girl or boy at camp would buy them for their very own and feed them peppermints by the handful. But that never happened. I didn't expect this place to be any different.

How long have you been here? I asked.

Goin' on six years, said Winnie. *I was one of them ponies that got trucked around to kids' birthday parties. Hard work, I can tell you, keeping a whole flock of sugared up young'uns entertained. Especially since half of them never seen a horse in their lives. One boy hit me with a stick 'cause he thought I was something called a* piñata. *He thought candy would come raining out of me. Brat had an arm on him, too. It wasn't usually so bad, though, except my fool owner didn't hardly feed me enough to keep flesh on a mouse.*

But I figured out that those frosted piles of grain with candles in them are the most delicious thing you ever did taste. I'd drag those weak little kids over to the table and help myself. That didn't go over so well with my owner, or the parents. I soon found myself at an auction with this real creepy man sizing me up to see how many pounds of meat he could get out of me.

Is that what happens to the horses who go to the slaughterhouse? I said, feeling sick. *People eat us?*

That's what I've heard, said Winnie. *Anyway, Lynn and Summer were there, and they rescued me. But not all the horses here came from auction. Devlan, the big chestnut, used to be a Grand Prix dressage horse. Then the stress got to him and he had some kind of meltdown. Started to rear and flip over backwards any time he got near a dressage ring. Now they use him for vaulting instead.*

I wanted to know more, but Chrissy let herself into the paddock and led Winnie away into the stable. The mare soon came out again all tacked up, led by a small girl wearing a purple riding helmet and matching breeches. Winnie craned her neck out in front of her and took mincing steps so that the girl had to practically tow her into the arena.

I watched the lesson with interest. Winnie, it turned out, had a few tricks under her saddle pad. When the girl used the reins to turn, the pony bent her neck like rubber and kept walking in the same direction.

In one corner, a patch of grass had spread under the fence.Winnie rooted her head down and tried to graze whenever she reached that spot. Every so often she'd drift to a halt in the middle of the arena and stand placidly while the girl kicked her tiny legs against the saddle.

She wasn't doing anything dangerous, but I was slightly shocked by her bad behavior. I was less patient with children than Opal, but I still usually tried to do what my rider told me.

Opal...just thinking about her gave me an ache in my belly like colic. Of all the horses in the world, Opal was the last who should have had such a terrible fate.

A lot of camp horses picked up habits like biting, cribbing, or rolling under saddle because they were underfed and overworked. They nearly always needed to see a vet and a farrier and have their teeth floated, and the lack of care made some horses mean. Others just stopped caring, and hardly even bothered to flick the flies from their bodies.

But Opal was always cheerful and well-mannered, even when the children forgot to fly spray her or pick the stones out of her hooves. If another horse chased her away from the feed tub, she'd give up her supper and forage for weeds instead.

I'm an easy keeper, she'd say. *Those big-boned hunter types need the oats more than I do.*

Maybe I could never be as good as Opal, but at least I could make myself too valuable to send back to auction. I would learn to jump like Falcon and float across the ground as gracefully as Devlan.

Opal was gone, I couldn't change that, but I could make sure I didn't end up the same way.

CHAPTER THREE

The Bargain

"Now ask Treasure to trot through the cones, Gracie," called Lynn.

I was in the middle of my first official lesson at Little Brook Farm. My rider was a six-year-old named Gracie. She was the girl in the purple helmet I'd seen having a lesson on Winnie last week. She had only started riding at the beginning of the camp session, and she was just learning to trot. She was still ironing out the finer points of steering, too.

Our riders were supposed to be guiding us in a zig-zag pattern down a line of six orange traffic cones spaced well apart. Unfortunately, Gracie steered me right toward the cones so that I tripped and knocked over each one.

After we had plowed through the exercise a few times, Gracie halted me in the corner while a more advanced rider, Emmy, jumped a course of small fences on a huge bay Clydesdale. Next to the arena was a grassy pasture in which several horses, including Falcon, were turned out.

As I rubbed my smarting foreleg with my nose, Falcon trotted over to the arena fence. I was surprised that Summer's prized jumper would take an interest in a beginner's lesson. Even just standing, Falcon was a sight to behold. His black coat shone like it was glazed with liquefied sugar. His lustrous tail nearly brushed the ground.

Good morning, Treasure, he said, nibbling on the top rail of the fence.

Hello Falcon, I replied, swishing my own, much less impressive tail. *What do you want?*

Oh, I just like to observe the children having their

lesson. It's nice that there are some horses at Little Brook who are suited for the purpose. Old horses, blind horses, ones with serious conformation faults. Not every rider is cut out to be a champion, nor is every horse. Yet every able hoof contributes something to the farm. It's sweet, don't you think?

I flattened my ears against my head. I wasn't old, or blind, and my swayback wasn't that bad—was it? Before I could reply by biting a chunk out of Falcon's perfect neck, Gracie kicked me forward to try the line of cones again.

As for me, I used to be a racehorse, so it's no surprise I would go on to have a second career as a jumper, Falcon called out as if he didn't notice he had just insulted me. *I've got the breeding for it—my grandsire is A.P. Indy, and my dam's sire is Storm Cat. Did you know I placed third in the Belmont Stakes as a three-year-old? The only reason I didn't stay in Kentucky to stand at stud was that I'd already been gelded. An insurance agent once estimated my worth at over a hundred thousand dollars.*

I wanted to reply that if I were a human, I wouldn't

trade a handful of moldy oats for a horse as arrogant as Falcon. But I was too out of breath from Gracie's uneven bouncing on my back. She hadn't quite got the hang of posting yet, and would often sit for two or three beats, then stand for one, then lose her balance and fall back into the saddle again. We approached the line of cones once more.

Summer used to do that exercise with me—back when I was practically a foal, said Falcon. *I used to pretend there was a little mousie trapped under each cone, and if I knocked it over, the poor thing would get squished.*

Thunk, thunk, thunk. I tried to avoid the cones, but Gracie was moving the reins all over the place. I could hardly keep my head straight, much less trot in a planned pattern. Soon every cone was lying on its side again.

EEEEE, squealed Falcon, so loudly that the other horses in the pasture looked up. *EEEEE, the poor mousies are being crushed!* Falcon stamped his hoof several times in appreciation of his own mirth.

That was it—I stopped in my tracks and refused

to budge. My mouth was sore from Gracie's constant tugging at the reins, even though Lynn kept urging her to hold the neck strap in front of my saddle if she felt off balance.

Gracie squeezed my sides with her heels, then kicked me, then made a loud clucking noise like a chicken. I didn't move. Lynn came over tapped my haunches with a riding crop. I hunched my back and bucked. Gracie shrieked and clung to my mane.

Lynn grabbed me firmly by the bridle. "Gracie, Treasure seems to be in a bad mood today," she said. "I'm going to have Summer bring her back to the barn and tack up Pie for you."

"Shouldn't Treasure keep working even if she's being naughty?" said Emmy. "Won't she learn she can get away with misbehaving if you stop the lesson early?"

"Sometimes that's true," said Lynn. "But Gracie hasn't been riding very long, and it's not safe for her to ride a cranky horse who might buck."

Summer untacked me and returned me to my paddock, then brought a blaze-faced quarter horse gelding up to the arena. He behaved beautifully for the rest of the lesson with Gracie. The pair even managed to get through the cones without knocking any over. I turned my nose to the corner to sulk.

I saw the whole thing, and don't you listen to a word Falcon says, Winnie advised. *That horse eats a big helping of corn-on-the-snob every morning with a side of brat mash.*

I wasn't really in the mood for Winnie's wisdom. I reached over and made a mean face at Duncan, who was foraging for sweet feed around my bucket. He ruffled his feathers and retreated with injured dignity.

The evening was clear and warm, so many of the horses stayed outside for the night. Lynn and Summer switched off the barn lights and went into the house. The horses drifted to the edge of their paddocks and stood as close together as the fences would allow. I flicked back an ear to listen, but didn't join them.

The big Clydesdale, Ben, let out a rumbling whinny. *Here at Little Brook Farm,* he called to me, *we have a tradition. When a new horse arrives, us old-timers go around and tell the stories of how we got here. Kind of breaks the ice.*

I turned reluctantly on my haunches to face the group. I wasn't in the mood for storytelling, but I didn't want to be rude. Falcon didn't seem to have similar worries. He snorted loudly.

If you all want to tell your sad sack rescue stories, go ahead, he said, *but Summer keeps me on a strict training schedule, and I need my recovery time. I'll be in the shed with my salt lick if anyone needs me.*

The black horse spun around and cantered with lofty strides over to the shelter in the corner of the pasture, where he began to suck on the edge of a large red mineral brick.

Good riddance, murmured Winnie, reaching down for a bite of hay.

I was a foxhunter before I came to Little Brook Farm, continued Ben as if there had been no interruption. *The country club ladies and gentleman would gallop me across the countryside. There was hardly a fox to be seen,* but everyone had a grand old time.

Of course, there were often more than a few flasks of brandy passed around during these rides. One day my tipsy rider crashed me right through a hedge in someone's garden. My check ligament was badly torn, and the club owners wanted to get rid of me at the first opportunity. Fortunately, I was rescued by Lynn. After I had rested for a few months I started my second career as a vaulting and lesson horse, with some competitive driving, too.

My story is a little different, said a mare named Hannah. She was so old that her hips were bony points on either side of her back. I was framed for murder!

I perked up my ears at that, and Hannah went on. My owner was a gambler, and he owed someone a lot of money. One night there was a loud argument inside the house. I heard a shot, then a stranger came outside, dragging my owner's body. He dumped it right in my stall. I was so frightened that I trampled it all over, trying to get away. By morning, it looked like I had kicked the man to death.

After they took away the body, no one knew what to

do with me. They decided I should be put down because I might hurt someone else. Fortunately, a young detective noticed the gunshot wound on the back of my owner's head, and my good name was cleared. Lynn saw the story about me in the newspaper and volunteered to give me a home.

I was so absorbed in Hannah's story that I jumped in my skin when a twig snapped under one of the horse's hooves. Winnie chortled, and I glared at her.

Unlike most of the horses and ponies here, I wasn't raised around humans at all, said a stocky liver chestnut gelding named Hamlet. His mane stood up in a brushy mohawk. I could see the imprint of a branding iron on his neck.

I was born and raised as a wild horse on the open ranges of Montana, Hamlet continued. *When I was three years old, men in helicopters rounded up my herd. They shipped me out East to a farm that sold cheap mustangs for a profit. But I'd hardly ever been handled, so I nearly broke the neck of anyone who tried to ride me.*

No surprise that I ended up at auction again. This

time the meat buyer was the only one who seemed interested. Even Lynn thought I was too wild. But Summer saw something in me and bid all the money she had.

For $800, just over my price-per-pound, she saved me from slaughter. Summer took her time gentling me with natural horsemanship instead of using whips or tie-downs to force me to do what she wanted right away. I came to trust her as I'd never trusted a human before.

I think that's how we all feel, said a striking leopard spotted gelding named Buddy. *Many of us never had a good owner before Summer and Lynn. I was shipped all the way to France to be ridden around a walled garden by a spoiled diplomat's son. When he quit riding to drive race cars instead, I was shipped all the way back. I figured it was my lot in life to be discarded like an old toy, as so many horses are when our owners get bored with us.*

Or when we can't handle the stress of competition anymore, added Devlan.

Or when we get sick and need extra care, said Pie, who wheezed and coughed if he didn't get his medication.

One by one, the rest of the horses told their stories,

from a wise old Morgan named Dallas who had lived at Little Brook for more than twenty years, to a shy pinto colt named Sebastian who'd been left to starve when his dam was taken away to nurse a valuable Thoroughbred foal whose mother had rejected him.

Some of the horses had been abused or neglected, and others had owners who loved them, but couldn't afford their care and had donated them to Little Brook. One mare had gotten lost in the woods after her trailer crashed on the highway, and had never been reunited with her owner. She had fallen in with a herd of deer and survived on her own for most of the winter before a family saw her roaming in their back yard.

Soon everyone was looking at me, waiting for me to tell my own tale. I shifted my weight uneasily. I didn't want to think back on everything I'd been through, but they had shared their secrets with me.

I was born in a farmer's field, I said finally. *For the first year of my life I ran free with my dam and two Belgian draft horses who sometimes pulled a wagon at county fairs. When my dam was younger, the farmer's*

47

daughter used her as a 4-H project.

Then the girl went away to college, and the old farmer retired. None of us horses had to work, we just grazed under the open sky through every season. When grass was scarce, the farmer drove a tractor down to the field and left a big round bale of hay.

My sire was an Arabian stallion who jumped his fence and went gallivanting around town, visiting the local mares. Apparently he was a prize-winning show horse with a pedigree that went nearly back to the dawn of time. His owner charged a lot of money for his stud fee, and was annoyed that the stallion had given away so many foals for free.

My dam was a thirteen-hand cob with no special breeding. I inherited most of my conformation from her, but she always said I had my sire's fine head and neck. When I was a weanling, the old farmer died and his land was sold. I was sent to my first auction, where I was separated from my dam.

My new owner was a spoiled teenage girl who hardly knew a thing about horses, except what she'd read in magazines. Her parents had built a small stable on their property so she could have a pony like she always wanted.

The grass in my new pasture was lush at first. But when I had eaten it all, my owner didn't feed me the right foods. She gave me table scraps as if I were a pig or a dog. I colicked twice. Eventually the family called out a vet who told them what I should be eating.

When I was only two years old, the girl would tack me up and make me gallop around the pasture. Sometimes she'd set up jumps and hit me with a crop to make me leap over them. I wasn't fully grown, and the girl was quite hefty for her age, so my back ached after she rode.

One day, the girl had friends over while her parents were on vacation. She brought them out to the barn to show me off. Her friends were drinking sour-smelling liquid out of glass bottles. They started to play loud music that sounded worse than a pack of howling coyotes. A boy flicked a cigarette butt into my stall, and the straw started to smolder.

My owner didn't notice, and a few minutes later all

the kids left in someone's car. The straw began to blaze and the flames spread to the walls. I tried to kick down the door, but it was too strong. I was trapped.

Luckily, a neighbor saw the smoke and ran into the burning building to let me out. I escaped with only a singed coat and a lingering cough, but from that day forward I could never step into another stall.

When the girl's parents returned and saw the charred rubble of the barn, they realized their daughter wasn't nearly responsible enough to own a horse. They sold me to a nearby summer camp. Unfortunately, it wasn't a very good one. The hay they fed me was more suitable for cows than horses. They never called out a farrier, so my hooves chipped and cracked from walking on the rocky trails.

But I liked the enthusiasm of the camp kids, even though they didn't know much about horses. There was one girl, Evelyn, who adored me. She would sneak out of her cabin at night and feed me carrot sticks she'd saved from lunch. She promised to take me home with her, but of course her parents said no.

At the end of the summer, when the kids went back to school, I was trucked to another auction. The camp would buy new horses again the next season, to save the cost of having to feed them over the winter.

For the next six years I was sent to six different camps. At first I got attached to my young riders, and felt sad when I had to leave them. But kids are kind of like horses. They have to do what the grown-up humans tell them to. I learned not to count on them.

As far as the other camp horses—well, I learned the hard way not to get too close to them, either. Except there was a gray mare at Camp Friendship, Opal was her name. She would share her hay with me when the bigger horses chased us away. At the end of last summer we were sold together in a bulk lot. I'd hoped we would stay together this year, too.

But Opal went lame before the auction. Stepped on a nail and got a high fever. She ... she ended up on the truck that takes horses away forever.

The other horses were silent when I had finished my story. The only sound was the soft hoot of an owl from beyond the dark border of trees.

It must have been awful, losing your friend, Winnie said finally. *And I can see why you'd take a powerful dislike to being trapped in a stall.*

Ben was watching me with his wise, calm eyes, but he said nothing. After my story, the gathered horses drifted away from the fence.

Although the mood in the paddocks was peaceful and my belly was full of sweet hay, sadness clung to me like smoke lingering after a fire. So many of the horses here had scars, or torn tendons, or sore backs from unkind or careless owners. Why did we keep trying so hard to please humans, even ones who didn't show the same concern for us?

I remembered a story my dam had told me when I was a foal who clung like a wild thistle to her side. *Long ago*, she'd said, *when men and horses still roamed the open plains, many dangers plagued them. Predators with sharp teeth stalked both horse and man, and starvation was a constant threat.*

One night, these first horses made a decision. They

approached the fires that the humans kept blazing all night to drive away the cold. Men had long hunted us for our meat, but they rarely caught us, for we were fast and strong. Now the horses lowered their heads and allowed the humans to place ropes made of woven river reeds behind their ears.

Fire had been our natural enemy, but that night the horses stayed close to the flames and listened to the drumming and stories. Human language was unknown to us, as ours was to them, but we saw that there was more to these creatures than the desire to hunt and kill.

The next morning, a bold young man approached the herd stallion—their names are lost to time—and flung himself onto the horse's back. The stallion took off running across the plains. He galloped so fast that his hooves hardly seemed to touch the earth, and he bucked so high that his heels nearly touched the clouds.

Caught up in the excitement of the story, I had broken away from my dam to gallop around the paddock, plunging and leaping as if I were trying to catapult an invisible rider from my back. My mother waited patiently until I returned to her side, then continued.

But the man did not fall. He clung to the stallion's back and let out a cry of sheer joy. Never had one of his kind been so united with the wind and the sky. Later, to thank the horse, the man gave him part of his meager ration of dried grains and berries. The pair discovered that both the food and the freedom were sweeter for having been shared.

That night, a bargain was struck between the two species. Forever after, men and women would shelter and protect horses. In exchange, we would share our swiftness by allowing them to ride on our backs. And the laws that we agreed on hold to this day: We obey their commands, we alert them to danger, we stay within their fences, and above all, we try never to harm them.

My dam had paused to look at me then, her eyes liquid and dark. I twitched my ears, listening for rabbits hiding in the long grass so I could pretend to be startled by them. I did not really understand what she was saying.

Over time, the strength of this bond has been tested,

my dam went on. *Humans have not always honored their end of the agreement. At times they have forced us to sacrifice ourselves in their wars and toil in their fields without adequate food and rest. We have given our lives and our foals to them, often with little thanks.* Here, my dam had reached out to brush her muzzle over the baby fuzz of my mane. I wondered if she knew that we would soon be separated.

Horses don't always honor the agreement either, she said, a warning note in her voice that made me forget my game with the rabbits. *We have abandoned them out of fear when they needed us most, and turned on them with angry hooves and teeth instead of remaining patient teachers.*

Yet on the whole we have tried our best to serve each other. We remain with men because that's the promise that was made by firelight so many generations ago.

So be good to humans, little one, my dam told me. *Teach them and learn from them. Because whatever happens, we are bound to them for as long as we live.*

CHAPTER FOUR

WINNIE AND THE CITY KIDS

A yellow bus pulled into the driveway and set the dogs to barking.

The city kids are here, said Winnie as the bus ground to a halt. *Brace yourself.*

The bus doors wheezed open, and children started pouring out of the vehicle. It was impossible to count how many. They didn't stay still long enough.

Some chased after the cats and some started climbing on the fences. Others ran around with no apparent purpose, shrieking like a flock of overexcited blue jays. One adventurous boy started scaling his way up the manure pile. A few adults who were with the children called for them to "find their farm buddies." No one seemed to be listening.

Summer entered the paddock and tried to slip a halter over Winnie's head. The cagey pony ducked her head and trotted away, tossing her head in amusement. After a brief game of keep-away, Summer cornered her near the water trough. Once she was haltered, Winnie heaved a sigh and followed Summer meekly. In the stable yard, the kids had been gathered into an almost orderly group.

I watched while Summer gave a grooming demonstration. She raised a cloud of dust from Winnie's fur with a curry comb, then swept her coat clean with a dandy brush. She showed the kids how to use a metal pick to clean the stones and debris from the pony's hooves. Chrissy brought out Winnie's saddle and bridle. The kids started to talk all at once.

"Do we get to ride the pony? I want to be first!" said a girl with a long chestnut ponytail.

"What if she runs away? I don't want to fall and get my outfit dirty." said her friend, brushing imaginary dust from her hot pink shirt.

"My uncle's a mounted policeman in the city," said a boy with a fierce expression. "I'm going to be one, too. I'll chase the bad guys on my horse."

Winnie seemed to view this boisterous group of childen as kindred spirits. She was surprisingly angelic while they took turns riding her around the yard. She didn't even try to scrape any of them off under the conveneint low-hanging branch of a nearby tree. But she couldn't resist hauling them toward a tasty morsel of clover now and then. And when she trotted, her bouncy gait nearly threw them out of the saddle.

I couldn't help but think that if it were me, I'd trot so silken smooth that even the smallest children would be able to keep their balance. But Lynn hadn't used me in a lesson at all this week. Was everyone still mad at me for trying the jump the fence with Gracie?

After the last girl climbed out of Winnie's saddle, a huge grin on her face, the kids ate their lunch at the picnic tables behind the barn.

People are lucky, said Winnie when Summer returned her to our paddock. *They eat all different kinds of food, not just hay and grain. Have you ever tried potato chips? They're nearly as good as Dr. Pepper, which—*

Suddenly Winnie's head snapped up. She trotted toward the corner of the paddock and hung her head over the children's picnic area. A moment later she spun around and cantered gleefully back to where I was standing. She dropped a brown paper bag onto the ground. *Didn't even see me take it*, she gloated.

You stole a child's lunch? I said in horror.

These kids sure are spoiled, replied Winnie, her nose deep inside the paper sack. *There's a whole apple in here...carrot sticks...ooh, a sandwich. I love PBJ.*

When Winnie finally came up for air, she had crumbs on her chin and her nose was smeared with purple jelly.

"Hey, someone took my lunch!" one of the children cried. He pointed over the fence. "That pony has it! She's eating my sandwich!"

Chrissy, who had just come out of the barn with a wheelbarrow full of dirty straw, ducked under the fence and pried the remains of the lunch out of Winnie's jaws. She handed the sack to its rightful owner.

"I don't think I want it anymore," the boy said, staring at the peanut butter dripping from the corner of the bag.

Chrissy smiled. "You can share my lunch today. I always bring an extra sandwich."

Winnie's ears perked up at the word *sandwich*. I snorted. Did that pony ever think about anything but food?

Once everyone had finished eating, Summer held a stall mucking and water bucket scrubbing demonstration, which was considerably less popular than the riding lesson. But all of the kids were willing to give it a try, even the girl who'd been afraid to get her outfit dirty. She perked right up when she saw there was a pink pitchfork that matched her shirt among the stable supplies.

After chores, the kids watched Summer ride Falcon.

They *oohed* and *aahed* as he cleared a course of fences that rose above most of their heads.

"I want to be a show jumper when I grow up!" said the girl with the ponytail.

"I bet we'll see Summer and Falcon in the Olympics someday," said the boy whose lunch Winnie had stolen.

I thought I felt a case of colic coming on. Didn't anyone see what a pain Falcon really was? Maybe he soared over the most daunting obstacles with ease, but he also fussed and fidgeted through the whole ride. He bucked after half the jumps, and shied at the cats who crossed through the arena as if they were mountain lions. He even tried to bite one of the children who leaned too far over the fence.

When the jumping demonstration was over, the teachers herded the kids back onto the bus. It took a long time because the boy who wanted to be a mounted policemen had chased some imaginary criminals into the hayloft, and no one could find him. Meanwhile, the girl in the pink shirt tried to sneak a litter of kittens onto the bus. After they'd gone, the farm seemed so *quiet.*

That evening, Summer and Chrissy took Ben and
me out for a trail ride. I was glad Summer wasn't riding
Falcon again. Ben walked companionably beside me,
his huge hooves clip-clopping on the packed dirt road
in front of the farm.

On the other side of the street was a building with a
group of people talking and dancing on the green lawn.
Someone was taking photos of a man in a dark suit and
a woman in a beautiful white dress. Everyone seemed
happy and excited. The music that drifted from the
party made my steps feel light and joyful.

Summer turned me off the road onto a trail through
the woods. Blackberry bushes lined the path, the berries
resting like dark gems against the leaves. I reached out
to grab a mouthful. The sharp thorns scratched my
nose, but the berries were juicy and sweet.

So how do you like living at Little Brook Farm? said
Ben as we walked under the dappled canopy of leaves.

It's wonderful, I admitted. *Nicer than anywhere else
I've lived. It's just—I sometimes feel like I don't belong*

here.

What do you mean? Ben edged over to one side of the path so that I could walk beside him more easily.

I'm not really good at jumping, or dressage, or vaulting like some of the horses here, I said. *I know others are old or lame and can't work much, and Lynn takes equal care of them all, but I want to be useful.*

The trail emerged from the woods to wind through a hilly meadow dotted with wildflowers. Our riders urged us forward. Ben broke into a lumbering trot, taking one stride for every two of mine.

You're good with the children when you don't let certain other horses distract you, said Ben. I recalled that he'd been in the arena the day Falcon had provoked me into nearly dumping Gracie onto the ground.

But I feel like it's not enough. I want to be talented like you, or Devlan, or... I trailed off.

Or certain other horses, Ben said drily.

At the top of the hill was an eagle's eye view of the valley below, a patchwork of dark green trees and pale green squares dotted with tiny sheep and horses. It was so peaceful up here. Even Summer and Chrissy, who had been chatting while they rode, fell silent at the sight.

I wouldn't worry about not being useful, Treasure, said Ben when our riders turned us back toward home. *I know Lynn is planning to let one of the campers enter you in the schooling show next month—if you behave until then.*

A show! I exclaimed. *Will there be ribbons and prizes?*

Well, yes, said Ben. *But it's not really the ribbons that are important, it's doing the best you—*

Will Falcon be showing too? I broke in.

Probably, said Ben. *But I always try to remember that doing my personal best is more important than—*

I didn't hear another word. Suddenly, I knew how I could prove that I was more than a swaybacked old lesson pony. I would beat Falcon in the show. I'd knock the bell boots right off his perfect hooves!

CHAPTER FIVE
CLYDE

The next few weeks seemed to flash by quicker than the flight of sparrows across the field. I grew accustomed to the daily routine of feeding, grooming, lessons, baths, and trail rides.

The regular campers had their lessons every day, and more groups of children came to the farm, too. Some wore metal braces on their legs or sat in wheelchairs, but they all seemed happy to be outside in the bright sunshine.

Lynn had started using me for lessons again, but never for these special groups. Gracie was my regular rider. At first she had crossed her arms and said "No, Treasure's mean!" when Lynn told her she was assigned to me for the rest of camp. She scowled the whole time she was brushing me.

When she leaned over to find a hoof pick in my brush box, I reached out to nibble the end of her braid. It had charmed Summer, and it seemed to work with Gracie too. She giggled as she pulled her hair free from my teeth.

"Maybe Treasure was just having a temper tantrum the other day," she said. "She doesn't seem so cranky now."

Gracie's riding had improved a lot since she'd started riding me. I liked to think that maybe I had something to do with it. She didn't hang on my mouth like before, and she usually remembered to post on the right diagonal. I knew there was no chance we would compete in the same division as Falcon at the show. But I could match him ribbon-for-ribbon by winning the championship in the beginner classes.

There were still two weeks until the competition,

and both campers and horses had been working hard to prepare. During lessons, the horses sharpened their responses to their riders' cues. They snapped up their knees over fences and softened their mouths to the bit.

The riders practiced their form too: heels down, back straight, eyes up, hands steady. They polished their tack until it gleamed. At some of the camps I'd been to, kids just handed the reins to stable hands when they were done riding.

Here, everyone had to learn horsemanship from the ground up. Nobody was allowed to sit on a horse until they knew how to groom one from nose to tail, and how put on our tack so that it fit comfortably.

They learned to place the saddle forward on our withers, then slide it back until it was in the correct position. They learned to tighten the girth slowly and check it just before mounting. They learned that a bit fit correctly if there was a wrinkle in the corner of the horse's mouth. If there were many wrinkles, it was too tight and would hurt the horse. If there were none, the bit was hanging too low and the horse wouldn't feel signals from the reins.

The riders learned all these things and a hundred more. Lynn insisted that riding didn't begin and end with sitting on a horse, and the campers were eager to learn.

But once in a while, someone made a mistake. On this particular afternoon, Gracie happened not to close the paddock gate properly after she turned me out. It swung shut behind her, but didn't latch. Gracie was too busy telling Emmy a funny story to notice.

Look at that, said Winnie, her eyes lighting up.

Don't even think about it, I replied. *We're staying right here and not—*

But Winnie was already gone. Quicker to find trouble than a hound on the scent of a fox, she nosed open the gate and trotted down the driveway.

Horses hate to be left alone. An itchy, fidgety feeling built up inside me. A moment later, I gave in and cantered after her. Gracie and Emmy had already gone into the stable, so the only witness to our escape was a tabby kitten rolling around on the driveway. Winnie chased her up a tree for good measure, then broke into a canter as she headed for the road.

Where are we going? I asked, breathless as I caught up to her. For such a pudgy pony, she could really move when she wanted to.

Mystery! Intrigue! Adventure! said Winnie, kicking up her heels.

We're going to be in a lot of trouble when someone notices we're missing, I said.

Cake!

What?

Winnie veered off the road toward the white building across from the stable. Once again, a crowd of people wearing fancy clothes had gathered on the lawn. I heard music like I had heard before, but this time it did not make my steps feel light and happy. It filled me with dread. I knew horses did not belong in the middle of this party, but that's exactly where Winnie was headed.

In front of the building, tables underneath a big white tent were loaded with food. In the center stood a magnificent three-tiered cake. *I've seen birthday cakes before, but never one that pretty*, said Winnie.

She trotted down an aisle between two rows of wooden chairs, then underneath a trellis covered in roses. Winnie paused for a moment, gazing at the cake with something like awe. Then she plunged her nose into the cream-covered pastry.

Bliss! Magnificence! said Winnie, snorting to clear the frosting from her nostrils. *Try some, Treasure. It beats sweet feed, hooves down.*

I hesitated. One bite couldn't hurt, right? I stretched my neck toward the remains of the dessert.

"AAAIIIIIII….!"

I shied sideways as a scream cut through the air. A woman in a long white dress was standing in the doorway of the building.

"Those ponies are eating our wedding cake!"

"I'll catch them, darling!" cried a man in a black suit who appeared next to her. He ran across the lawn toward Winnie. She backed away from the cake and into one of the other tables. Red liquid sloshed out of a crystal bowl. Winnie leaped forward and got tangled up with a wooden chair. She kicked viciously until it collapsed and fell to the ground.

The woman in the white dress had found a wreath of flowers. She moved steadily toward Winnie, holding the wreath over her head like a lasso. I wasn't sure whether she was planning to catch Winnie with it or strangle her.

Time to go! said Winnie, bolting back under the rose arbor. Clods of grass and dirt flew from beneath her hooves, leaving deep grooves in the ground. I caught a last glimpse of the shocked faces of the crowd before I clattered after her across the road.

When we reached our paddock, Winnie slipped through the gate, skidded to a halt, and assumed a sleepy expression. She cocked one hoof as if she were resting. Thirsty after my gallop, I drank deeply from our water trough.

Act real casual when they come for us, she murmured, blinking lazily.

What do you mean, "when they come for us?"

A moment later, the woman in the white dress

and the man in the black suit stormed into the stable yard. Lynn came outside. She looked puzzled while the couple yelled at her. Finally, everyone came over to our paddock.

Lynn looked from the open gate, to me, and then to Winnie. The pony's eyes were closed and she was all but snoring. Lynn glanced back at the man and woman with a doubtful expression. Then she squinted at Winnie's chin. The jig was up. Clinging to Winnie's long whiskers were the crumb-and-frosting remains of the beautiful cake.

I thought it was too bad that we'd been chased away before I had a chance to try it myself. Was it really better than sweet feed? How could anything be better than sweet feed?

What have you two gotten into now? said Ben, looking sternly down at us from his imposing height. *I saw you bolt out of here a few minutes ago. Don't you have any respect for the law of fences? We don't go through them unless someone's leading us!*

It was my idea, not Treasure's, said Winnie, licking

the frosting from her whiskers and managing to look guilty and satisfied at the same time. *And it was really Gracie's fault for leaving our gate open...*

What happened? asked Hamlet, trotting over to the fence. By now, most of the other horses had gathered curiously at the edges of their paddocks.

I was just planning to go up to the hill, maybe have a nice after-dinner graze, said Winnie. *But there was this scrumptious cake outside on a table, just begging to be eaten. Then a woman in a fancy dress saw us and chased me with a wreath of flowers.*

They were getting married! said Hannah. *I used to pull a carriage when I was just a filly. I was quite the high-stepper back then, and I saw lots of people dressed like that. You just ruined that poor lady's wedding.*

Winnie scuffed the dirt with her hoof. *People shouldn't leave cakes sitting out if they don't want ponies to eat them,* she muttered. Then she groaned.

I don't feel so good...

You're probably going to colic, Falcon said smugly.

For the rest of the afternoon, Winnie stood bellyaching in the paddock.

I hope you've learned something, said Ben.

Can't talk, said Winnie, *dying*. She swayed on her hooves.

I was concerned for my paddock mate. I whinnied until Summer and Chrissy came out of the stable. They watched Winnie nip at her swollen belly.

"It looks like colic," said Summer. "We should call Dr. Fallon." She led Winnie out of the paddock and made her walk in circles around the stable yard until the vet arrived. Winnie tried to drop to her knees and roll, but Summer wrestled her back to her feet. If horses rolled when they were colicking, they could rupture their gut and die.

Fortunately, the vet arrived quickly. She poured some slimy medicine down Winnie's throat, and Summer kept her walking until she passed manure. It was a sign that Winnie was out of danger. Summer kept her moving for another half hour, then put her in a stall for the night. I felt sorry for the greedy pony, but I was glad she hadn't *quite* tempted me to try the cake.

Winnie was back to her old self the next day, although she showed considerably less appetite than usual. There was no camp on weekends, so the farm was quiet until mid-afternoon, when I heard the crunch of tires on gravel. Lynn's trailer rattled up the driveway. She and Summer had left early that morning after packing the trailer with hay nets and refilling the first aid kit with bandages, sedative shots, and antibiotic cream.

They got out of the truck and began to unlatch the back of the trailer, their faces grim.

Looks like there's going to be a new addition to the herd, said Winnie.

When the door swung open, a powerful stench hit my nostrils. I could see a set of gaunt hindquarters inside the trailer. Summer ducked into the front and I heard her speak soothingly. The horse's stick-thin legs trembled. It took a step back, then another, and gradually emerged into the light of day.

The gelding was little more than a skeleton covered

in copper fuzz. Flies swarmed over his weeping eyes and running nose. His hooves had grown so long that they curled up into a spiral, like grisly sled runners.

Worst of all was the horse's expression. The muscles around his mouth twitched with tension, but his eyes were glassy. I wondered for a moment if he was blind, but saw him flinch away when Summer reached toward his face to brush away the flies.

It took a long time for the horse to shuffle into the barn on his overgrown hooves. I stared after him in shocked silence.

Don't think I've ever seen a horse in such bad shape, Winnie said finally. She seemed to be searching for one of her colorful expressions, but for once failed to find one.

I bet they'll call the vet and have him put to sleep, said Hannah. *It's sometimes the kindest thing when a horse is in so much pain.*

Dr. Fallon's truck turned into the stable yard just a few minutes later. But she did not put the horse to sleep. For two weeks the gelding stayed in the quarantine stall. Hannah, who usually spent the night in the barn, told us that he never said a word. Sometimes he would have strange fits in the night, squealing and kicking the walls.

Hannah thought he had probably been locked somewhere alone for a long time, so long it had made him lose his mind. Maybe he had even been shut away somewhere since he was a foal, and had never learned horse or human language.

He had a name, though: Clyde. It was engraved on a dirty gold plate on his moldy halter. Once, someone had cared enough about Clyde to have his name inscribed on his tack. I couldn't help but think that it must have been a very long time ago.

After the worst of his sores had healed, Clyde was moved to a stall in the main barn that opened into a small paddock.

At first he just lurked in the doorway, his eyes glinting in the shadows. Finally he stepped stiffly outside and stood in a patch of sunlight. Even though a farrier had trimmed his awful hooves, he moved like he had concrete blocks attached to his legs. The white patches on his ribs and belly didn't look like natural markings, but places where old injuries had healed over.

Hello, Ben called out, his welcoming nicker sounding a bit thin. *Welcome to Little Brook Farm.*

Clyde didn't answer. He didn't even seem to notice us watching him. Suddenly the gelding turned and started viciously biting his own side. His coat darkened with blood and bits of fur floated to the ground.

Then, as suddenly as he'd started his attack, Clyde stopped. He stood with his lip drooping.

I think someone done hollowed out that horse's head and filled it with hornets, said Winnie, rolling her eyes nervously in Clyde's direction.

For the rest of the day Clyde stood in his paddock, as motionless as if he were carved from stone. He didn't eat his hay, or drink from his water trough, or even flick his ears when any of the horses tried to engage him in conversation.

At feeding time, Summer opened his stall door and poured his evening grain. Clyde's ears flattened against his skull and I could swear I saw his eyes glint red.

He barreled inside and charged at Summer. She slammed the door just in time. Clyde gouged the wooden door with his teeth and kicked the stall wall so hard that blind Casper in the next stall whinnied in a panic, thinking the barn was collapsing.

Clyde dug his teeth into the grain and tossed his head, sending a splatter of sweet feed into the straw. Duncan watched from a safe distance, clucking with disapproval. Even he wasn't foolhardy enough to go after that windfall.

Clyde ended up flinging more of his grain into the air than he ate, even though he seemed desperate for food. When he was finished he stood in the stall rocking his weight from side to side, a vacant look in his eyes.

I didn't feel very hungry for my own grain that evening. I was glad Clyde had been rescued from his terrible prison, but I wondered if a horse that broken could ever recover.

CHAPTER SIX

The Show

The children arrived early on the morning of the schooling show. The dew hadn't yet dried from the grass when Gracie stumbled sleepily out of her mother's car. I had been bathed with bubbly, flower-smelling soap the day before, but I had rolled in the dirt to get the scent out of my nose.

Gracie groaned when she saw me, then grabbed a bucket of water and a rag to wipe me down as best she could. She had braided my mane yesterday, but the yarn made my neck itch so I had rubbed many of the braids loose.

Gracie chatted with Emma while she worked. The other girl had Ben tied to the paddock fence while she picked out his huge hooves. I was used to the cross-ties by now, but there wasn't enough room to bring me inside today. Everyone wanted a space close to the tack room to get their horses ready.

Most of the lesson students were here, dressed in tan breeches and black or navy hunt coats over white show shirts. Gold or silver stock pins gleamed at their throats. The older riders wore knee high field boots, while the younger ones wore ankle height jodhpur boots. A paint mare named Lyric was showing in the Western division, and her rider wore a fancy embroidered shirt and a cowboy hat.

Gracie's mother had French braided her flyaway blond hair, then tucked it up under her black velvet show helmet. It made her look more grown up than usual. Gracie spritzed something from a spray bottle onto my coat. It smelled nicer than fly spray and made my fur feel slippery.

"Don't put any conditioner on Treasure's back, or

her saddle might slide sideways," warned Emmy. She stood on a three-step mounting block to braid Ben's forelock.

The only horses who weren't being ridden in the show were old Hannah and Dallas, blind Casper, and the minis, who were too small. And Clyde, of course. Even with all the excitement around him, he stood as statue-still in his paddock as ever, his eyes fixed on some invisible object or memory in the distance.

At least he didn't bite his side so often, and the sores on his ribs were starting to heal. Still, it was hard to tell if he recognized any horse or human, or if he even noticed that he was no longer trapped alone in whatever darkness he'd been rescued from.

Gracie applied a coat of clear polish to my hooves. I wrinkled my nose at the smell. Horses from neighboring stables began to arrive in trailers. The air rang with whinnies of greeting and challenge. Lynn walked past carrying a box full of multicolored ribbons.

"Your halter class starts in fifteen minutes, so you should head up to the arena soon," she said to Gracie.

"You'll be in the walk-trot division. After the halter class you have equitation, pleasure, and ground poles."

"Are those the prizes for the winners?" said Gracie, peering into the box of ribbons. "If I win, I'm going to take a pink one. It's the prettiest color."

"The winner always gets a blue ribbon," said Lynn. "Red is second place, yellow is third, white is fourth, pink is fifth, and green is sixth."

"I changed my mind then," said Gracie. "I definitely want a blue ribbon."

Lynn smiled. "Remember that Treasure should be wearing her bridle for the first class, but no saddle because you'll be leading her. You should be wearing your helmet, and don't forget to shine your boots."

I stood impatiently while Gracie buckled the straps on my bridle. I nearly dragged her up to the arena. A dozen horses were already waiting by the gate. Inside, the judge was looking over the horses in the Western halter class. Lyric looked very pretty in her fancy show bridle with jewels on the browband. I wasn't surprised when the judge called her forward to receive the blue ribbon for the class. Even though I hadn't won the ribbon myself, I felt a surge of pride on behalf of the farm.

Gracie's mother came over and pinned a square of white cardboard with a number on it to the back of her jacket. She pulled a handkerchief out of her pocket and wiped the dust off her daughter's boots. My nose itched, so I rubbed it against the fence, which Lynn had stained a few days ago in preparation for the show. It felt sticky on my face.

"Oh no!" said Gracie, "Treasure's got a mark from the fence on her blaze."

Her mother scrubbed at my nose with her handkerchief, but didn't seem pleased with the results.

Summer and Falcon came prancing over. Falcon jigged impatiently in place while Summer looked over a jump course posted outside the arena. Falcon looked even more magnificent than usual with his mane done up in dozens of black button braids. He already had a blue ribbon clipped to the headstall of his bridle.

Won my conformation class a few minutes ago, he

said, tossing his head to make the ribbon flutter. *I'm heading to the warm-up ring now to get in the perfor-mance zone for my working hunter under saddle class.*

Congratulations, I said, grinding my teeth on my bit.

With that swayback of yours and those unfortunate cow hocks, it's brave of you to enter a halter class, he said. *The judge will be looking at your conformation as well as your grooming and turnout. By the way, there's a smudge on your blaze.*

I chomped harder on my bit. Summer signaled Falcon to walk on, and he strutted confidently toward the temporary grass arena where several riders were practicing over fences.

That horse really cools my bran mash. Didn't his mommy ever teach him any manners?

I turned on my haunches and saw Gracie's friend Charlotte leading a shiny roan pony. It took me a moment to realize it was Winnie. I hardly recognized my paddock mate. If there was anything in the world that Winnie liked better than food, it was wallowing in a patch of mud. She was usually crusted with dried soil and dyed with grass stains, but now she gleamed nearly as brightly as Falcon. I hadn't even realized that Winnie had two white socks underneath the grime that usually covered them.

The arena gates opened and the horses from the Western class filed out. The English horses took their place, lining up in the center of the ring. The judge was a bald man wearing a tweed coat. He walked down the row, examining each of the horses in turn. He frowned when he saw shavings in Buddy's tail, and made a note on his clipboard when he noticed Pie pawing impatiently at the ground.

The judge walked in a circle around me, his sharp eyes seeking out flaws like a hawk searching for a juicy mouse. He brushed a hand over my coat and ran his fingers through my tail. No snags there—Gracie had brushed it into a silky cloud.

The judge asked each horse to walk to the end of the ring, then turn around and trot back. I had never seen the point in trotting anywhere you could reach as easily by walking, but today I broke into a jog as soon as Gracie tugged my reins. I tried to float across the ground like my Arabian ancestors had floated across the sands of the desert.

After all the horses had shown off their gaits, the judge's assistant came into the ring with a rainbow of ribbons lined up on a piece of cardboard. Gracie fidgeted nervously beside me.

"First place in the walk-trot in hand class goes to number forty-seven, Mackenzie Hale and Gold Dust," said the judge.

A red-haired girl and a glossy palomino from another farm stepped forward to accept the prize. The second place ribbon went to Emmy and Ben. Third place was given to another horse I didn't know, and Winnie took fourth.

The judge clipped the pink ribbon to my bridle. Gracie had gotten her favorite color after all. Last place, the green ribbon, went to Buddy. The shavings in his tail drifted down like snowflakes whenever he swished at a fly, and his braids stuck up at weird angles.

I tossed my head as Gracie led me out of the arena,

enjoying the feeling of the satin ribbon fluttering from my bridle. So we hadn't won, but I was sure we'd do better in the riding classes. Anyway, the pink ribbon *was* the prettiest color.

Falcon came strutting over. Just my luck, Summer halted him next to me to talk to a rider from another farm about a training clinic they were both interested in.

Fifth place, eh, Treasure? Falcon said in a patronizing tone. *Well, it's better than being last, I suppose.*

Summer was holding a second blue ribbon in her hand. Suddenly the pink ribbon on my own bridle didn't feel so special.

Gracie reached up to pat my neck. "Good girl, Treasure," she said. With the under-saddle classes coming up, I couldn't help wishing she were a better rider who never bounced on my back or tugged my mane for balance.

Gracie put on my saddle, got a leg up from Lynn, and we headed back into the show ring for equitation. This class judged the rider's form. The judge asked the horses to walk and then trot in each direction. Then we had to halt on the rail and back up six paces.

Except Gracie was pulling harder with her left rein than her right, so I thought she was asking me to turn around. I nearly bumped into Winnie as I shifted my hindquarters sideways, confused by my rider's instructions.

I wasn't surprised when we were given the green sixth place ribbon. Dead last! If only someone like Summer would ride me, I might have a chance at winning the blue.

In the next class, walk-trot pleasure, the judge was looking at the horse's performance. The winner would be the one with the smoothest gaits and the most obedient responses. I was determined to win. I walked so smoothly that my hooves hardly raised a puff of dust. I did a perfect turn on the forehand to change direction. I snapped my pasterns at the trot and kept my ears pricked forward. I didn't even cough when Ben's huge hooves paddled dust into my face.

The judge called the horses into the center of the

arena and asked us to back up again. This time, I knew what was being asked, and I backed so straight you could have used my path to plot a fence line. I stood without moving a muscle while the judge made his decision.

"First place in the walk-trot pleasure class goes to Emmy Silversmith riding Ben."

I didn't hear a thing after that. I felt like my head was filled with buzzing bees. I stepped forward automatically when Gracie nudged me with her heels and leaned down to accept the red ribbon.

Second place? Didn't the judge see how Ben had stumbled when Emmy asked him to trot? I ducked my head low as I walked out of the ring, ignoring the other horses' congratulations.

The final class, ground poles, was a disaster. Gracie got confused by the figure eight pattern and ended up taking me over the last two poles in the wrong direction. Nonetheless, she beamed proudly when her mother took a photo of us holding her green sixth-place ribbon. I must have ruined the picture, because I kept my ears flattened in annoyance. Didn't she care that we had come in last place again?

Back at the barn, Gracie sponged me off with a bucket of soapy water and let me graze on the lawn. She fed me an apple, and I couldn't help nuzzling her hair affectionately. Gracie might not be a great rider yet, but she was improving. Maybe in a few years she would be as good as Summer.

Still, I felt a pang of envy as I glanced over at Falcon. He was preening while Summer's friends snapped photos and stuffed him with carrots. Six sleek blue ribbons hung in a row on his stall door, and Summer was holding the glittering golden championship trophy for her division.

I wondered what it felt like to be a champion, like Falcon. I wondered if I could ever do anything that was worth so many prizes.

CHAPTER SEVEN

Hard Lessons

"Now circle around and try the cross-rail again, Gracie."

It was a hot, dusty afternoon a few weeks after the show. I had been trotting over the same jump for what felt like a century. Gracie kept letting her leg slide back so that she fell forward onto my neck when I jumped the small fence.

"Heels down and eyes up!" called Lynn. Immediately I felt Gracie's heels bounce up and her head tilt down. Her hands gripped the reins and I slowed obediently to a walk. Gracie kicked me forward. I was so confused from the mixed signals that my legs got tangled in the fence and the crossed poles went crashing to the ground.

Lynn sighed. "Remember that you need to look where you want your horse to go, Gracie. Let Treasure rest for a minute and we'll try it one more time. Emmy, you can take Ben over the vertical line, then do a roll-back to the barrel jump. Remember to keep a strong leg and spot your distance."

I walked over to the corner of the ring and stood while Ben took his turn jumping. I envied the horses grazing in the cool green pasture next to the ring. As if on cue, Falcon detached himself from the herd and wandered over. At that moment, Duncan fluttered awkwardly up onto the fence post. Great, now I had the company of my two least favorite animals on the farm.

Did you hear that Summer's taking me to a training level event next weekend? Falcon bragged.

Duncan made a low, impressed, birdy sound. I pulled at the bit, trying to get enough rein to push the rooster off the fence, but Gracie just tugged back in response.

Only training level? I said. *I'd have thought that an amazingly talented jumper like you would be competing at the advanced level by now.*

No, no, said Falcon, bobbing his head in false modesty. *Eventing is an all-around sport, requiring the discipline of a dressage horse as well as the power of the jumper. As you know, I have no problem with the latter, but the haute école is still new to me. My breeding is for raw speed rather than finesse. When I placed second in the Belmont Stakes, I never even considered that I might someday piaffe and passage my way to a championship.*

I thought you placed third in the Belmont Stakes, I said.

It was a photo finish, Falcon said vaguely. *I don't recall if it was second or third. Anyway, my dressage training with Summer is quite intense. I'm having some delayed muscle soreness from the lateral work, but I think that—*

I turned my hindquarters toward Falcon and Duncan, pretending to watch Ben jump. I just wasn't in the mood to hear about how Falcon was planning to set the fastest cross-country time ever recorded, jump higher than any horse in history, and get a silver statue of himself put in the stable yard so that everyone would know the amazing Falcon lived here. Maybe Lynn would even rename Little Brook Farm and call it Falcon Brook Farm instead.

Summer jumped me over that fence this morning, said Falcon, bobbing his head toward a huge red-and-white striped oxer set up in the middle of the ring. *She said it's four feet, six inches high. Of course, that's not nearly as high as I could jump if I wanted to, but Summer is careful not to over-face me while I'm still maturing. Got to stay sound if I'm going to make it to the Olympic Games.*

I just grunted and reached down to take a bite of clover. It turned out to be sour-clover. I spit it out. Gracie tried to pull up my head, but she wasn't strong enough to stop me if I really felt like grazing.

I see you're jumping today too, said Falcon in a patronizing tone. He glanced at the cross-rail I'd been trotting over for the last half hour. *Good for you.*

95

"Something's wrong with Treasure," Gracie called as I stamped my hind leg several times. "She seems angry."

"She's just annoyed because Falcon is standing so close to the fence," said Lynn. How perceptive of her. "It's your turn to jump, anyway. Remember to keep your weight in your heels and release with your hands."

I trotted toward the little *x* and lumbered over it. This time, Gracie grabbed a handful of mane so she didn't pop me in the mouth, but she lost her balance and fell forward onto my neck. The extra weight made me hit the rail with my foreleg. The pole was solid wood, and my cannon bone smarted from the contact.

If you'd care for a professional tip, said Falcon, *imagine that the jump poles are actually live snakes. It might stop you from having so many rails down.*

That was it—I'd had enough! I was sick of Falcon's snobby advice, sick of giving lessons to wobbly beginners, and most of all I was sick of cross-rails.

Gracie turned me down the quarter line of the ring for the thousandth time. But instead of trotting obediently over the tiny fence, I grabbed the bit in my teeth and bolted. Gracie shrieked and clung to my mane. I could feel her slipping sideways in the saddle. Lynn tried to corner me, waving her arms, but I swerved around her.

I was headed for the red and white oxer in the center of the ring, the one Falcon had jumped. It was bigger than anything I'd ever attempted, but I was determined to make it over. If I did, it just might shut Falcon up once and for all.

I headed for the oxer at a flat-out gallop. But as the jump rushed closer, I realized just how high it loomed. I shifted my weight onto my haunches, then slammed my hooves back into the ground. Gracie sailed over my head and landed in the dirt on the other side of the jump.

I kept going to the far corner of the arena—away from the oxer, away from Lynn, away from Falcon, away from everyone. I wished I could jump the arena fence, but it was even higher than the one I'd just refused.

I could hear Gracie crying. Lynn rushed to her

side while the other riders halted their horses and dismounted. Ben looked at me disapprovingly from across the arena. I glared back at him. What did he know? He went to vaulting competitions with Devlan, which was nearly as impressive as being a show jumper. He didn't know how it felt to have everyone think that you weren't good enough for anything but cross-rails.

Still, I felt guilty as I heard Gracie's sobs. What if I'd hurt the little girl? I had certainly broken my end of the bargain between horses and humans. *We obey their commands, we alert them to danger, we stay within their fences, and above all, we try never to harm them.* The long-ago words of my dam echoed in my head.

Of course, all horses spooked sometimes and threw their riders, but to do so deliberately was different. It was much worse. I walked back over to where Gracie had fallen, my head hanging low. Lynn had taken off her helmet, and the girl's face was streaked with dirt and tears.

"Go away, Treasure," Gracie said as I approached. "I don't like you anymore!"

Maybe it was just a coincidence that Duncan chose that moment to let out a loud, triumphant crow.

"You should get back on if you're not hurt, Gracie," Emmy called out. "Otherwise you'll be afraid to ride again."

"I'm not getting back on," said Gracie. "I'm no good at riding. I quit."

"Don't be a chicken!" said Emmy.

"Well I *am* hurt," said Gracie. "I think my arm is broken. I need to go to the doctor right away."

Lynn looked skeptical, but she just said, "Okay, Gracie, I'll call your mother and have her come pick you up." She glanced over at me. "It's time for the lesson to end anyway. Emmy, can you untack Treasure and make sure she's cooled off?"

Back at the stable, Emmy left me on the cross ties while she untacked Ben. The sweat that had dried on my coat felt itchy and uncomfortable, and my legs were sore from all the galloping. The cool water Emmy sponged onto my coat felt nice, but it didn't make me feel better inside.

WHITNEY SANDERSON

That was bad, *Treasure,* said Winnie in a tone of shocked admiration when Emmy returned me to the paddock. *Even I've never done anything that bad.*

I didn't say anything. I hadn't meant to hurt Gracie, I was just sick of being good. I was tired of having the smallest, bounciest kids ride me all the time. Horses like Falcon got riders like Summer because they were too difficult for anyone else to handle.

But horses like Falcon were also more valuable than I was. The only reason Summer put up with Falcon's antics was because he was such a good jumper. Sway-backed lesson horses like me who misbehaved got sent to auctions. Even though Ben said that none of the horses here were ever sold, I wasn't sure I believed it.

Ben was eating his hay in the paddock next to mine. I walked over and nickered to get his attention.

What is it, Treasure? he asked, lifting his massive head.

Are you sure that even really bad horses who get rescued don't get sent back to the auction?

Ben gave me a level stare as he chewed his hay. *They*

100

won't send you back to auction, he said finally. *But they might not use you in lessons any more. A few of the horses here aren't ridden because they do dangerous things like rear or bolt.*

I turned away from my own pile of hay and paced my paddock nervously. Had I just ruined my chances at being a lesson horse? Would anyone ever trust me again?

CHAPTER EIGHT

Second Chances

Gracie didn't ride me in her next lesson. She switched over to May, a new pony who'd been rescued from a petting zoo. I was surprised to realize that I missed my young rider, bouncing heels and zigzag steering and all.

The older kids didn't like riding me because they all wanted to jump higher than cross-rails. The younger kids were still afraid of me, even though I had never run away with another student after Gracie. I wasn't anyone's favorite anymore—Gracie seemed to like May a lot. When I saw her hugging the pretty dark bay mare after her lesson, I felt like I'd been sprayed in the face with a cold hose.

I trudged my way through lessons as if I were pulling a heavy bale of hay behind me, and flicked my tail irritably at my riders' signals. Lynn started using me less and less. Most of the time I stood in my paddock with my back turned to the activities of the farm. Even Winnie's cheerful schemes to supplement her diet with human treats seemed more annoying than amusing now.

One gloomy gray afternoon that matched my mood, a maroon van pulled into the driveway. Two adults helped four children out of the back seats. I had seen kids like this before, with some problem that seemed to make their muscles too rigid or too soft. Often, these children moved with the help of metal leg braces or crutches.

Or, in the case of one boy, a wheelchair with a strap crossed over the front of his body to keep him from falling forward. He couldn't even hold up his head, which seemed too large for his delicate neck, like a

103

baby bird's.

One by one, Summer led each of the children around on Winnie. The pony picked her way reluctantly through the mud puddles from last night's storm. The children's expressions were not like the animated faces of other humans, but tense and still. It was hard to tell if they were happy or frightened or sad. They seemed lost in worlds inside their own heads.

A girl with rainbow beads braided into her hair hummed a song to herself and played with Winnie's mane while she rode. Her aide asked if she wanted to hold Winnie's reins herself, but the girl only looked away and started rocking in the saddle. Winnie backed up nervously and bumped against the fence, then scooted forward.

The aide quickly pulled the girl down off the pony's back. The girl went over to sit on a nearby bench. She walked with crutches, her small legs twisting sideways with every step.

The bench was near Clyde's paddock. The gelding was standing with his hindquarters in the stall and his front legs outside. He seemed unwilling to move fully into the daylight or retreat entirely into his stall. Somehow his stiff body reminded me of the children who were having their lesson.

Finally it was time for the boy in the wheelchair to ride. Lynn and the boy's aide, a young woman, unfastened his harness and lifted him out of the chair. He was like a ragdoll in their arms. They tried putting him on Winnie, but she skittered away at the sight of his floppy arms and legs. They tried putting him on Ben, but they couldn't lift him high enough. Buddy and Hamlet were also too nervous, and the only other small pony, May, had a sore leg.

"Why don't we try Treasure?" said Summer. "She's not much bigger than Winnie."

"I don't know," replied Lynn, "she's been acting out of sorts lately. I'm not sure if she would be safe."

"Maybe we should just take Michael back to the bus," one of the aides said quietly as the boy let out a shout of frustration. I noticed that Clyde, standing halfway between his stall and the paddock, flicked an ear toward at the sound.

Please, I thought. *Please give me another chance.*

"Okay," Lynn said finally, as though she had heard my thoughts. "Bring Treasure out."

Summer led me out of the paddock and slipped on my bridle, but didn't bother with a saddle. "I think it would just get in the way," she said to Lynn.

"The heat of the horse's back might help Michael relax," said his aide.

"Are you ready, Michael?" said Lynn. She smiled, but her eyes looked sad. The aides lifted the boy out of his wheelchair again. Lynn helped maneuver his right leg over my back.

Even though he was small, he felt heavier than many of the kids who rode me. His weight settled differently on my back, and he didn't give me any signals with his seat and legs. It felt strange, like I was suddenly moving around without one of my senses. I was used to my rider telling me what to do, and shifting their weight to match the rhythm of my stride.

Summer asked me to walk on. I hesitated, feeling like

the boy would topple right off my back. She clucked to me and I stepped gingerly forward. Lynn walked on one side and the boy's aide walked on the other, steadying him.

I stepped to the right to avoid a puddle. Michael leaned dangerously to the left. Part of me wanted to bolt, but instead I focused on putting one hoof in front of the other as carefully as I could. Lynn helped Michael balance upright on my back again. Another puddle loomed ahead. This time I splashed through it instead of moving to the side.

After three circuits of the yard, Summer asked me to halt. The aide slid Michael off my back and helped him into his wheelchair. She rolled the chair forward so it was right in front me. My instinct was to move away from the strange contraption, but I made my hooves stay planted like trees in the ground.

Michael's aide lifted his hand and placed it on my neck.

"This is Treasure," said Lynn. "This is the horse you rode for the first time."

Michael's aide moved his hand down my neck, then through the rougher hairs of my mane. Lynn put a carrot in his hand.

A smile flitted across the boy's face when he felt my breath on his palm and heard me crunching the carrot. The expression was as fleeting as the rainbows that sometimes appear in the dewy air after a summer storm. Even when it was gone, a kind of light seemed to stay in his eyes.

I noticed that Falcon was watching over the fence. For once he wasn't chewing on the rails or making some rude remark. He craned his neck toward Michael, then changed his mind and backed away. He whirled around and galloped to the far end of his paddock. He dropped his head and began to graze, tearing up large tufts of grass.

But I could see the white corner of his eye, and I was sure he was watching while the aide helped Michael run a brush down my neck. She had to hold her hand over his to keep the wooden brush from falling to the ground. I wondered what life must be like for a boy who couldn't even reach for things he wanted.

When it was time for the children to leave, all three the staff members had to help position the boy in his car seat. While they were busy, the girl with beads in her hair got up from the bench. She stood in front of Clyde's paddock and made a soft two-note chirping noise, like a chickadee's call.

Clyde was watching her. Something seemed to gather in his eyes that had been absent before. His muscles tensed. His ears flickered crazily in all directions, as if he were being given a million different signals at once.

The girl climbed through the boards of the fence, pulling her crutches through after her. Clyde's muscles tensed, then relaxed. He took one hesitant step toward the girl, then backed up, then suddenly trotted over and stopped dead in front of her.

I was afraid the unpredictable gelding might bite, but he only sniffed up and down the girl's body as if she were another horse. The girl spread her tiny hand flat over the white star on his face. Clyde closed his eyes and lowered his head nearly to the ground.

The girl's aide finally noticed that she had wandered into Clyde's paddock. She ran over, looking frightened. "Cara, what are you doing? Get out of there before that horse hurts you!"

People came hurrying to help. Lynn started to let herself into Clyde's paddock, but stopped when she saw that Clyde didn't seem upset by the girl's presence. He he was resting one hind leg, something I had never seen him do before. His jaw softened into a rhythmic licking and chewing motion as Cara ran her hands over his face. This is how horses show trust, a gesture left over from the earliest days of their lives.

Cara was talking to Clyde in a song of made-up words. His ears flicked more quietly now in response. The pair stayed like this for minutes that seemed to shimmer outside of ordinary time.

"Amazing," said the girl's aide. "She's never shown an interest in another person or animal. She has autism. I can't imagine what the world must be like for her. I think it's very loud and bright. Most of the time, it seems like she just wants everyone around her to go away. That must be some special horse."

Cara's pressed her hands to the sides of Clyde's face and said something that no one but she and the gelding could understand. Then she took hold of her crutches and climbed awkwardly back through the fence.

She avoided the curious gazes of the adults who were watching, but her face shone with the same secretive smile as Michael's. It was as if Clyde had just told her a wonderful story. Surely it wasn't the tale of his life—but what, then?

Clyde's gaze followed Cara until she was inside the van. She stared back with her hands pressed against the glass. The van pulled out of the driveway and disappeared. Clyde shook his head as if he were clearing cobwebs from between his ears. He took a deep breath that made his whole body shudder. Then he arched his neck and looked in every direction with soft brown eyes, as if he were seeing the place for the first time.

He trotted clumsily over to his water trough and blew ripples across the surface. He splashed and played with the water before drinking. Ben nickered another greeting to him. Clyde looked at the draft horse with a curious expression, then ducked his head shyly and blew more bubbles into the water.

I wasn't sure that Clyde would ever be normal, but at least now he seemed more like a horse than some eerie creature that was used to living in a shadowy cave. I didn't know exactly how it had happened, but it seemed like the locked stall in his mind had finally opened to release him.

The leaves were starting to take on a tinge of autumn color and bitterness when the last session of camp ended. Michael came back to the farm three times, and on each trip his eyes looked a little more alert to the world around him. He held a brush by himself now, and he had learned the sign-language symbol for carrot. I learned it too: Someone making a fist as if they were holding a carrot, then moving it closer to their face while they pretended to crunch the imaginary treat.

Cara visited with Clyde while the other children were riding, and it seemed as if the withdrawn child and the strange horse were continuing to heal each other somehow.

Lynn had started using me in regular lessons again. There was a new swing in my stride, a new quickness in my response to my riders' instructions. Gracie started riding me again while May recovered from a stone bruise to her hoof. Today we'd had a clean round over a course of eight cross-rails, and I even managed a flying lead change.

I understood now that working with the youngest children was not a task left to the least useful members of the herd. Only the steadiest, most patient horses could be trusted to take the first steps with a new rider. Horses could have a special talent for it, the way others might be gifted at jumping or dressage.

Other animals on the farm seemed to notice my change of attitude too. One day while I was standing with my rump to the fence having an afternoon siesta, I heard a weighty flutter behind me and felt scaly feet on my back.

I bucked in alarm, which only caused the claws to

dig in. The animal was in my blind spot, but surely I was being attacked by some vicious bird of prey! Maybe a real falcon instead of the equine version. I bucked again, but the creature only bounced on my back and cackled in alarm.

Calm down there, bronco, it's just Duncan, said Winnie.

Sure enough, when I craned my head around to look, I saw the rooster perched on my hindquarters, glaring at me with his fiery yellow eye.

Take it as a compliment, called Dallas, snorting with mirth. *Duncan only perches on his very favorite horses.*

Sure enough, Duncan stayed planted on my back until feeding time. Then he retired to the ground with a feathery flop and waited expectantly near my feed tub. I wasn't quite as careful as usual about cleaning up every morsel of my grain, and Duncan feasted happily on my leftovers.

You're going soft on us, Treasure, said Winnie with a twinkle in her eye.

I just don't have much of an appetite tonight, I said

gruffly. *I had a big flake of hay at lunch.*

Sure, said Winnie, rolling her eye skeptically in my direction. *And I'm on a new diet where I don't eat anything but oat bran, because I'm watching my fillyish figure.*

I reached out and nipped at the air in Winnie's direction. She reared up with mock fear, and I chased her in a few circles around the paddock until she became winded and refused to move.

A big horsefly was buzzing around her head, so I moved over next to her and offered to swish it away with my tail. She lowered her head gratefully, and we stood nose-to-tail to keep the fly at bay. Meanwhile, Duncan settled into a corner of my shed to roost.

On the last day of camp, the riders celebrated with a picnic on the hill where I had taken my first trail ride with Ben. Lynn and the campers drove ahead in the pickup truck, leaving Summer and Chrissy to finish the evening chores.

When the last stall was mucked and the last water bucket filled, the girls tacked up Falcon and me.

Couldn't Summer have ridden Hamlet instead? But not even that could spoil my day, with my latest triumph over cross-rails and the memory of Michael asking to feed me a carrot.

The black gelding was unusually quiet as we walked. I expected him to start bragging about the three-day event he'd gone to this weekend. A huge red, white, and blue championship ribbon was hanging on his stall. Or maybe he would spin and bolt back to the stable, which he often did around suppertime.

Instead, he said something that surprised me.

I didn't really place in the Belmont stakes, you know. In fact, I was never a racehorse at all.

Falcon mouthed at his bit and kept his gaze trained on the road. Why was he telling me this? Maybe he was going to reveal that he was actually descended from the royal stallions of Argentina or something.

My dam was a Thoroughbred, he continued, *but I spent the first year of my life in a tiny pen fenced with barbed wire. My dam starved herself to make sure I got a fair share of whatever coarse straw or stale corn our owner occasionally brought us. She said I was a growing colt and I had more need of it.*

I took it and demanded more. I was hungry all the time, and it made me greedy. There was grass growing on the other side of the fence. One day I bolted right through the barbed wire, trying to reach it. Someone saw me tangled up in the fence from the road.

Falcon halted suddenly and itched his face against his foreleg for a long time. Then he trotted ahead of me so I could only see his glossy hindquarters. I was as startled as if someone had emptied a washbucket over my head. I'd figured Falcon had been treated like he was made of solid gold for his whole life. But he was a rescue, like me. My heart ached when I thought of him as a weanling foal so desperate for food that he would charge a barbed wire fence.

Falcon laid back his ears as I trotted to catch up to him. *But I'm not just some fleabag rescue,* he said. *I can jump almost five feet, and I'm going to be an advanced level eventer.*

You're very talented, Falcon, I said honestly. *Much*

more than I am.

At jumping, maybe, said Falcon. He tossed his head up and down a few times to make his curb chain jingle. I'd noticed that he did this when he was nervous, as if the tinkling sound calmed him. Of course, I'd also speculated that he just did it to be annoying.

But Lynn and Summer trust you with the children, Falcon went on. *With the fragile ones who come on the buses. They don't trust me like that. They always shut me in my stall or turn me out in the back pasture so I won't bite or accidentally knock one over. Sometimes I wonder what it would be like to have one of the little ones ride me. I guess even Summer started out that small, riding gentle ponies who wouldn't scare her.*

Falcon suddenly seemed embarrassed by everything he'd said. He jerked his head and pretended to spook at a passing butterfly. He bolted up the hill while Summer hauled back on the reins and yelled at him to behave.

At the top of the hill, Lynn had set up a striped tent to cover picnic tables loaded with fruit salad and corn on the cob. It reminded me of the wedding party I'd attended not so long ago. But Winnie was back at the stable, so the food was safe from her marauding schemes. The camp kids raced around, laughing and pretending to canter like horses.

My nostrils flared in alarm when I smelled smoke from the barbeque pit, but I relaxed when I saw that the fire was contained. Gracie offered to hold me while Chrissy got something to eat. The little girl picked a handful of lacy white wildflowers to braid into my mane.

Nearby, Summer was sitting cross-legged on the ground while Falcon grazed. She had removed his tack, and I saw what I had never noticed before—thin scars from barbed wire running down his legs and belly.

The grass was lush, but I didn't feel like eating. I gazed across the valley below. The landscape was divided by many roads that disappeared over the horizon. Somewhere out there was the place I had come from, and the place where Opal had gone. Even though the horses at Little Brook Farm had become my new herd, I still missed Opal's wise presence and her reassuring warmth in the night.

119

"Hey Gracie, Lynn said we can play mounted games on Treasure!" cried Emmy, running over. "She brought helmets up for everyone."

Summer boosted Gracie up onto my back. The campers took turns in a relay race against Summer and Falcon. We had to gallop to the end of the meadow, wait while our riders gobbled a piece of watermelon, and gallop back.

By the last leg of the race, Falcon and I were neck and neck. His long legs flashed beside me as the finish line approached. Then—maybe it was just a trick of the light—it seemed that Falcon's eye twinkled. A moment later he shied sideways, and I surged across the finish line first.

"We won! We beat Summer!" The children gathered around and threw their arms around me, not minding my sweaty coat. Someone fed me a piece of watermelon. I looked over at Falcon. He was standing aloof as the children crowded around us. Had he really been spooked by something, or had he let me win the race?

Gracie held out a piece of watermelon to Falcon,

flat on her palm.

"Careful!" said Summer. "Falcon nips sometimes."

Falcon looked uncertainly at the piece of fruit in the girl's hand.

Try it, it's delicious, I said, my own mouth dripping with juice.

Falcon stretched out his neck and delicately took the piece of watermelon.

"Good boy," murmured Summer, sounding surprised.

"Can I hold him?" said Gracie. "I think he likes me."

Summer hesitated. Falcon was standing still for once, and he lowered his head to let out a whooshing breath through Gracie's hair. Summer smiled, then replaced Falcon's bridle with a halter and handed the lead rope to Gracie.

For the rest of the evening, Falcon and I grazed while the campers took turns holding us. Falcon was docile, not even flinching when a firefly landed on his nose and lit up like a tiny lantern. Normally he skittered away in disgust if another horse came too close, but tonight he allowed me to graze beside him. It was hard to believe that a horse so full of boasting and bravado had once been a frightened weanling too weak to escape the pen that held him prisoner.

I snorted to signal to Falcon that I'd found a patch of wild clover. He moved closer to share it with me. His proud, wild eye had softened in the twilight, although he twitched off the hands of the children who were trying to braid flowers into his mane.

I guess he needed to draw the line somewhere, but I knew now that Falcon and I were not as different as I'd thought.

CHAPTER NINE

OLD FRIENDS

The season of sweet meadow grass faded into the season of crunchy leaves and no more stinging flies. Snow fell, and Summer and Chrissy taught me to drive a sled. I trotted around the plowed paths surrounding the farm, bells jingling festively on my harness. Summer and Chrissy seemed to have a lot of fun giving rides to the younger children, although they ended up in a snow bank a few times after trying to turn the sled too sharply.

The spring thaw came, and the kids tapped the maple trees around the farm for syrup. They collected buckets filled with a few inches of watery sap, which they boiled into a tiny, cloudy jar of maple syrup. They carried this prize all around the barn to show off. Unfortunately they left the container too close to Winnie's stall, and were deprived of the pancake breakfast they'd planned to celebrate their labor.

Nice, but I prefer molasses, said Winnie, licking the syrup off her whiskers.

The April sunshine melted the ice and warmed our shivery backs. The air was scented by new grass and lilacs. Camp started when the grass began to taste baked by the first heat of summer.

Life at Little Brook Farm was a new adventure every day, but somehow reassuringly the same. Lynn moved around the farm with the energy of a whirlwind, teaching students, organizing shows and clinics, fixing broken fences and leaky troughs. Amid all this, she somehow kept up with the endless feeding, watering, and mucking out. Every so often, she and Summer would rush out with the trailer to bring back another member for our herd.

One day they returned not with a horse, but a white hen named Tootsie who quickly moved into my shed with Duncan. Seeing the strain on my goodwill that feeding two large birds caused, Winnie generously began sharing some of her own grain with our fowl friends.

Somehow another year slipped by, then five, then five more. Despite the comforting familiarity of the farm routine, there were signs of the time that had passed. The barn looked a little less red each year, each winter seemed to make my joints stiffer. One day old Dallas, who had lived at the farm for more than thirty-two years, couldn't get to his feet one morning. He was put painlessly sleep by Dr. Fallon, surrounded by many of the riders who had loved him.

As for my other old friends, most of them hadn't changed much. Winnie had grown stouter and lazier than ever over the years, and concocted ever more devious plans to trick people out of their lunches. Falcon had become an accomplished jumper who won many prizes. His temper mellowed, but he always kept some of his arrogant swagger. He still took great pleasure in standing by the paddock fence at lesson time, squealing like a little mousie whenever I knocked over an orange cone.

Summer trained more promising young horses, and Hamlet became such a talented eventer that a member of the Olympic equestrian team who visited the farm offered to buy him. But Summer couldn't part with the gelding she'd rescued from the meat buyer for $800.

Although Lynn sometimes matched a horse with a new owner, Ben had been truthful when he said that none were sold or sent away to uncertain fates. The gentle draft horse was still ambassador to every new arrival, although his muzzle had gone gray and he set down each giant hoof even more slowly and deliberately than before.

Clyde was still different from other horses. He often lurked and circled in his stall, and he never made a sound. But he had stopped biting his own flanks so viciously that he added to his old scars. He nearly always stood near the fence when a van or school bus pulled into the yard, although he didn't take the same notice of the children who ran around the farm every day.

It seemed like his gaze always fixed on the child who lashed out at his helper, or who was locked away inside her own head. Sometimes it seemed like these children got calmer when they noticed Clyde watching. It was as if something unexplainable passed from the strange, silent gelding to the children no one else could seem to reach.

I liked working with these children best, too. I never grew tired of seeing their anxious faces relax into smiles when they felt my whiskers tickling their palm to accept a carrot. They seemed to look at the world with a new confidence when they realized they could use their hands, legs, and voices to make me move where they wanted.

Emmy and Gracie grew into teenagers and excellent riders. A new generation of beginners, complete with shiny new boots, bouncing seats, and unsteady hands, had taken their place. They didn't know a forelock from a fetlock, but they'd learn soon enough.

Outside the safe haven of Little Brook Farm, times were hard. Calls came in from people who couldn't afford to feed their animals. Once in a while, a family would find a "wild" horse stealing birdseed from their backyard feeder because a desperate owner had led the horse out into the woods to fend for itself.

One day Summer and Lynn drove off with the trailer, which meant a new horse would be coming. Gossip jumped from paddock to paddock. Hamlet thought Summer might be adopting a new mustang, and Falcon had heard that a fancy lesson barn had gone bankrupt, leaving a dozen A-circuit hunters homeless.

Near suppertime I saw headlights in the driveway. I flared my nostrils, trying to catch a scent. There was something familiar that I couldn't quite place. Lynn opened the trailer door and a lean mare backed out. Her coat was a warm cream color that stirred something in my heart and memory. Then she spotted me, raised her plain head high, and whinnied a long forgotten greeting.

Opal!

The air rang with my joyful neigh. Unable to gallop over to her as I wanted to, I wheeled in two quick circles and struck the gate with my hoof. The noise startled the chickens, descendants of Duncan and Tootsie who had carried on tradition by residing in my shed. They cackled and milled around the paddock, bumping into each other and flapping their wings in surprise.

Opal still had perfect manners. She did not drag Summer over to greet me, but only leaned hopefully in my direction and nickered to me again.

Summer could tell that something unusual was happening, and she brought Opal over to my paddock. I bumped noses eagerly with my old friend, blowing out my breath in a whoosh of welcome.

How did you get here? Are you well? Where have you been, all these years? When you were led away by that man, I thought...

Opal rumbled low in her throat, amused by the questions running like water from an overflowing trough. *I am safe, and you are here,* she said. *That is all that matters now—there will be time for stories later.*

129

Summer led Opal away to the shed on the hill where I'd spent my first weeks here. The wait would be a torment, with all my questions unanswered. But at least I could see Opal, who was making friends with one of the cats. Watching her, I could reassure myself that her appearance wasn't just another dream that would evaporate like morning dew when I awoke.

Opal must have seen a veterinarian recently, because she didn't have to wait two weeks for her Coggins test results like I did. Dr. Fallon checked her over the next morning, then Summer brought Opal to the paddock I still shared with Winnie.

At last! I cried as she was turned loose. *Come, a victory lap!*

I nipped playfully at Opal's withers. We must have been a funny sight, two old mares trotting in circles around a flock of chickens. Our knees flashed high as we fell into step beside each other. It didn't matter that Opal hitched on one foreleg, or that my strides were short and stiff. We might as well have been Lippizaners performing airs above the ground.

Some of the newest lesson kids brought out flakes of hay and an extra bucket of water. "I wonder why Treasure and this new mare are so crazy about each other," said Jordan. "Maybe they were born in the same stable or something."

"That's silly," Andrew replied. "Horses don't remember each other like people do."

"How do you know?" Jordan demanded. "You're not a horse—you just smell like one, haha!"

The discussion ended with the two kids chasing each other around, waving riding crops. Lynn called out to scold them from inside the barn, somehow knowing without seeing them that they were up to mischief.

Opal and I were left alone in the paddock. We settled down and had a bite of hay together while the other horses gathered to hear Opal's story.

There were twelve of us in the meat buyer's truck, said Opal, after she had explained about the camps, the auction, and the nail that had lamed her. *I was wedged into the trailer between an old gelding who couldn't chew* his hay anymore, and a Thoroughbred colt with a bowed tendon. We could smell the fear and sickness from the horses that had been there before us.

When the auction was over, the driver headed for a highway. We could hear other huge trucks roaring past, and the floor vibrated under our hooves. We were driven all day, through the night, and on into another day.

The trailer stopped from time to time, but no one came to check on us or give us water. The sun beat down on the metal roof and made it hotter than a blacksmith's kiln. On the second day, the old gelding dropped down dead from fear and exhaustion. The rest of us had to pack together to keep from stepping on him.

Come nightfall, we stopped in front of a building that pulsed with loud music. I fell into a doze and woke up to the sound of a siren. Through the slats in the side of the trailer, I saw our driver being led toward a car covered in flashing blue lights.

Then an even brighter light swept over us. I heard a voice say, "There's about a dozen horses here that look to be in pretty bad shape. I know it's late, but try to reach

Joan at the ASPCA."

Soon, a few smaller horse trailers pulled into the parking lot. People with gentle voices and hands led us out one by one, until only the dead gelding was left. More people came flooding out of the building, drawn by the flashing lights.

They were laughing at first, but they got quiet when they saw the gelding being dragged out on a tarp. "How could anyone be so cruel?" cried a woman tottering on glittery heels bigger than the fancy shoes they put on Tennessee Walking horses.

Someone else said, "I got a pasture with an old shed about a mile from here. It's nothing fancy, but these poor creatures are welcome to spend the night there."

Some of the horses resisted getting on the trailers again, now that they were back on solid ground. But I could tell these people meant to help us, and I was too tired to put up a fight. I was brought to an overgrown paddock with a rough shelter, and given food and water. My leg hurt from the nail and my body burned with fever. I was afraid I had lockjaw.

I had seen horses with this terrible disease before, so stiff and trembling they couldn't even swallow their own saliva. The only thing a vet could do at that stage was give them a shot to mercifully end their life.

Opal went on. *Then I remembered that one camp, a few years back, gave all the horses some needle jabs at the beginning of the session. I just hoped that I'd been given the right one to protect against infection from the rusty nail.*

The next day, the humane society vets cleaned out my hoof and gave me another injection. Within two days the fever was gone. Soon after, they found a home for me.

I lived in a hilly field with a cozy barn that I could go in and out of as I pleased. My owner was a kind snowy haired woman who lived in a yellow cottage at the top of a hill. She fed and watered me twice a day, and often stayed to brush me and talk to me while I ate.

In the summer, her grandchildren came to visit and rode me all around the field. I limped from the nail wound, which never really healed, but the children didn't mind. It wasn't a bad life, but my days were lonely with no herd and only the wild rabbits and butterflies for company.

After many years, the my owned died, and I was even more alone. A neighbor came to feed me from time to time, but it wasn't always enough. My ribs started to show through my fur. Just a few weeks ago, a pair of strangers came and loaded me onto a trailer again.

I feared the worst when I looked out the window and saw streets filled with cars and big buildings. I thought for sure that I was being taken to the slaughterhouse. But we passed through the city, and there were hills and trees again.

I won't be afraid of trailers anymore, Treasure, because that one brought me here.

Opal looked around at the cozy paddocks, the freshly raked ring with jumps set up for tomorrow's lesson, and the barn closed up for the night. Nothing was fancy or showy, but there was a feeling of belonging here that was different from anywhere else I'd known. I wondered if Opal could feel it too.

It's hard to believe you ended up at the same farm as Treasure, after being separated at the auction so many years ago, said Winnie, chomping contentedly on a dandelion blossom that had made the mistake of growing too close to our paddock. *That just takes the wedding cake.* The pony gave me a sly look.

You don't need to worry about being lame, Opal, Falcon said with surprising gentleness. *The horses here give lessons or enter shows if they can, but you won't be forced to carry riders if it pains you.*

Opal bobbed her head shyly. *I hope I can. I love children, and it sounds like there are many of them here.*

Yes, I've always loved children myself, said Falcon, curving his neck into a graceful arc and pawing lightly at the ground. Was he flirting with Opal? I coughed to hide my snort of laughter.

The other horses soon began to doze, but I was wide awake. For all these years I had thought Opal was gone forever. How lucky she was to have escaped the fate that awaited so many unwanted horses.

Opal, I said. *You knew the trailer at the auction was going to the slaughterhouse, you could smell it. Why did you get on? Why didn't you rear or kick or run away?*

Opal lifted her head and chewed a mouthful of hay

thoughtfully. Her dark eyes reflected the nearly full moon.

Horses have to go where people lead them, she said in her simple way.

I knew she didn't just mean that someone would have caught her and forced her onto the trailer in the end. She was talking about the bargain that was struck between horse and man so long ago, under the light of the same moon that shone on us now.

Horses have to go where people lead them. Sometimes we are brought to dark places far from the sweet grass and the sun. We never know whether the next hand that grasps our lead ropes will be cruel or kind. Still, we do our best for our owners, because they are bound to us as we are bound to them.

Opal moved over to graze beside me. A breeze blew across the paddock and twined the strands of our tails together, white and black.

I felt like a harsh bit that had been pressed into my mouth for a long time had finally released. Had the grass always tasted this sweet? Had the barn always looked this lovely in the moonlight? Opal herself gleamed so soft and silver that she could have been a unicorn from a foal's tale.

Horses have to go where people lead them, but sometimes we are lucky. Sometimes we find ourselves grazing with an old friend under a summer moon. We end up safe and loved, knowing we will always be cared for. Sometimes we are lost for most of our lives, but eventually we find our way home.

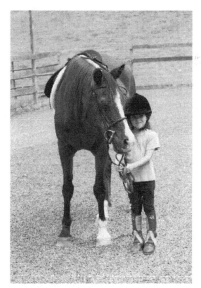

Treasure—the real pony who inspired this story—

and a special friend at Little Brook Farm.

APPENDIX

ABOUT HORSE RESCUE

Every year, more than 100,000 horses and ponies in the United States are sent to slaughter. They are often shipped long distances to Canada and Mexico under inhumane conditions. Many more horses in the United States are abused or neglected every year. They may become old or injured and no longer considered useful, or they may have loving owners who do not have the resources to care for them.

Some industries contribute directly to the problem of unwanted horses. Thoroughbred racing stables often fail to secure long-term homes for retired racehorses, although some farms make an effort to responsibly place horses leaving the track. Even one Kentucky Derby winner, Ferdinand, ended up going to slaughter in 2002. On PMU farms, mares are deliberately bred so that medical products for humans can be made with their natural hormones. Many of the foals who are born on these facilities end up homeless.

Fortunately, there are stables all across the country (and in other parts of the world) that offer sanctuary for equines in need. These rescue agencies provide food, shelter, and medical care. They may also rehabilitate injured or poorly trained animals to become lesson or show horses, and adopt them out to new owners.

There is no single organization that oversees horse rescues, so it is important to know the history of any farm where you might want to volunteer or donate money. You should ask how long they have been open, how many animals they have rescued, where they have been placed, and how they fund their operation. You should also make sure that the animals look well fed and cared for, that the shelters and fences are well maintained, and that the farm has a vet and farrier who routinely examine the horses. Many farms that rescue horses also take in other animals in need, such as cats, dogs, rabbits, donkeys, and different kinds of livestock.

Most horse rescues welcome volunteers and scheduled visitors. If you are interested in becoming involved, you can check online or call your local chapter of the ASPCA to see if there are any horse rescue farms in your area. There are always horses that could use a human hand, and your help matters!

About Therapeutic Riding

People with physical, developmental, and emotional disabilities can benefit from riding and working with horses. The side-to-side motion of a horse's gait mimics the motion of walking, and riding can help increase the strength and balance of people who cannot stand or walk on their own. People who find it hard to control their mood or behavior can build confidence and self-control through grooming, handling, and communicating with horses.

Some people who do equine therapy can ride on their own, but others need leaders or side-walkers to assist them. Therapeutic riding lessons often involve games and activities like horseback basketball or Simon Says to help people improve their balance and ability to signal their horse. More importantly, these games are fun!

Many people with disabilities can learn to ride as well as able-bodied people, although their horses may need to learn to respond to different cues. In 1952, Lis Hartel from Denmark won a silver medal for dressage in the Olympic Games even though she was paralyzed from the waist down by polio. Her story sparked interest in therapeutic riding techniques, and the North American Riding for the Handicapped Association was founded in 1969. The organization is now known as PATH International, and has more than 850 centers across the world.

Therapeutic riding began with people who had physical disabilities like cerebral palsy or spinal cord injuries. More recently, equine activities have been shown to help behavioral and emotional disorders like autism and attention deficit disorder. Sometimes people who have trouble communicating or staying focused at home or in school will see improvement in these areas when they start working with horses. Therapeutic riding typically involves mounted activities, while equine assisted psychotherapy often uses ground work to help people learn effective communication and coping skills.

It takes special horses and ponies to do equine therapy. They must have good manners, friendly temperaments, and not be easily spooked or upset. Therapeutic riding horses are given special training that includes being mounted from either side, standing still when someone leans on them for balance, falls, or drops something under their feet, and working around specialized equipment like crutches and wheelchairs.

Therapeutic riding programs are often in need of assistants to groom and tack up horses, lead or side-walk during lessons, and do stable work. Helping out at a therapeutic riding program is great way to get volunteer experience, meet new people, and get in some horse time.

About Little Brook Farm

Lynn Cross began rescuing horses when she was only sixteen years old. She opened Little Brook Farm in 1977 after she returned from college, making the 55-acre farm in the countryside of Old Chatham, New York the oldest horse rescue in the United States. Since then, Lynn and her daughter Summer, along with the dedicated staff, student interns, and volunteers at Little Brook farm, have provided a safe haven for hundreds of horses, ponies, and other animals.

In addition to providing sanctuary, the farm offers community riding lessons, horsemanship camp, clinics, and shows. Summer trains horses and competes in eventing on her gelding Hamlet, who she rescued from slaughter. In 2013, she adopted a paint mustang named Amado through the Bureau of Land Management and competed in the Extreme Mustang Makeover challenge.

Lynn is the founder of a nonprofit educational program, Balanced Innovative Teaching Strategies, Inc., which pairs students with equine partners to help build the trust, skills, and confidence of each. B.I.T.S. often hosts field trips at Little Brook Farm where children from urban schools can experience farm life for a day, helping to groom and feed the horses and play in the famous hay bale maze. They also offer therapeutic riding, where children with disabilities can benefit from riding and working with horses.

Little Brook Farm currently cares for 70 horses and two donkeys, as well as many cats and dogs. Some of their rescued animals are placed in carefully chosen homes. Others, like Treasure, remain at Little Brook for the rest of their lives.

The farm has provided safe haven for many breeds of horses from different backgrounds, including ex-race-horses, jumpers, dressage horses, camp horses, draft animals, carriage horses, and family pets whose owners are no longer able to care for them. Many of the rescued horses have gone on to compete successfully in dressage, jumping, team vaulting, and other events.

Little Brook Farm rescued Treasure, a part-Arabian pony mare, from a slaughter auction in 2001. The other equine characters in the story are also fictional versions of real horses from the farm. Treasure was a patient teacher and beloved favorite of many young riders until she passed away in 2013, around the age of 25.

To learn more about Little Brook Farm, visit their website at www.thelittlebrookfarm.org

ABOUT THE AUTHOR

Whitney Sanderson decided to write a story based on the life of Treasure after she spent a summer volunteering at Little Brook Farm in 2010. Whitney is the author of *Horse Diaries #5: Golden Sun* and *Horse Diaries #10: Darcy*, two titles in the popular chapter book series published by Random House. Another book for young readers, *Harlequin: The Story of a Circus Horse*, will be released in 2015, along with a second Horse Rescue story.

Whitney started riding when she was six years old, and has shown in 4-H, hunter-jumpers, and eventing. She has a chestnut snowflake Appaloosa named Thor whose favorite activities include going on trail rides, napping in the pasture, and eating peppermints.

To learn more about Whitney's books, visit
www.whitneysanderson.com

Made in the USA
Middletown, DE
23 June 2015